FORGETTING, REMEMBERING, REACHING

Rufus Rawls

CONTENTS

INTRODUCTION

This book, *Forgetting, Remembering, and Reaching,* will enhance the seeker's spiritual growth when received with an open and hungry heart. Moreover, it will provide a fresh biblical perspective of the precious spiritual benefits of fulfilling the purpose of this book by applying the discipline of *forgetting, remembering, and reaching.* Given that the total of salvation includes forgiveness, healing, prosperity, deliverance, safety, rescue, and liberation, the believer's spiritual growth and maturity in Jesus Christ begins by developing and perfecting the discipline of *forgetting, remembering, and reaching.* This transformation will likely involve facing unpleasant and challenging memories, situations, and experiences. Even so, it is a necessary route to forgetting the past, remembering the promises of God, and reaching deeply within your heart with the determination not to look or desire to go back.

However, knowing exactly where you are going is difficult until you get there. But neither the present promises of God nor His future glory can be held hostage by cherished memories or past regrets. Nevertheless, precious time is often ignored, and the growth potential is hindered until this important truth is understood – *back* is not *back* there! In other words, the past is just that, past.

If a hungry heart is thirsty for righteousness and embraces this book with hallowed expectations, the experience will be similar, yet different from that of the 120 in the Upper Room. Neither the gatherers in the Upper Room nor the massive crowd in Jerusalem for the feast knew beforehand what was going to happen until the day of Pentecost had fully come. Although the Galatians were speaking in an unknown tongue to the multitude (Acts 2:1-8, every person in the crowd understood what was being said in their native language.

Your needs are, in a sense of speaking, foreign to everyone but you. The Holy Spirit ministers to you personally and intimately based on your sincerity, faith, calling, growth, and your desire to know and experience His presence. However, He will not necessarily bless you with what you want or believe you need. He will bless you according to what God has purposed for you. The Holy Spirit desires to teach you three important principles in particular: How to forget temporal things, remember the promises of God with the courage and determination to reach deeply into your heart and embrace the glorious plans God has for you.

To this end, expect to be empowered with the courage to forget past defeats, the discipline to resist wanting to relive past victories, and the foresight to view the present as a single rung on the staircase of life that is constantly ascending into the future. The Spirit of Christ will teach you how to proclaim and reach for the promises of God with the assurance that they are your rightful inheritance. Hence, the believer who practices these disciplines will master the ability to resist the temptation of clinging to past fears or desires. Once this crafty distraction is recognized and resisted, your deliverance will become a surefire source of unrestrained joy, strength, and liberty.

This book, *Forgetting, Remembering, Reaching,* includes a brief narrative of the apostle Paul's life. If you can identify with specific events in your spiritual journey through his, it will help you identify where you are, and to realize that your walk of faith either begins or continues from where you are. If you desire to develop a closer walk with God, learn to walk in the now realm of faith. This book provides simple, yet practical solutions to the following closely related questions: What are God's plans for me? Where am I now on my spiritual journey? Where do I need to be? How can I get there?

However, discussing forgetting and remembering from different viewpoints in this book is not an attempt to group conflicting ideas together. But by gaining insight into the essential steps of *forgetting, remembering, and reaching* prepares you to retire the past, and instills hope for the future from within the brief reality of the present.

Meantime, though, please remember your time and timing are much different than God's. And since the last days began with Jesus's birth, you are now possibly living in the last hour of the last day in this dispensation of grace! In preparation for His imminent return, God is equipping the end-time saints with a fresh anointing to disarm and destroy the works of the devil. When and wherever the perfected or the maturing love of Christ is missing, the frustrating presence of fear, hurt, regret, and lusts of the flesh will continue to rule and hold the soul hostage until the glory of God is enthroned in each obedient heart. Therefore, holy readiness requires *forgetting, remembering, and reaching* for the power of Christ that is available to each of us as we labor in the vineyard of God while treading the turbulent waters of life.

Listen to the apostle in 1 John 4:18 for inspiration to press forward: "There is no fear in love [dread does not exist], but full-grown (complete, perfect) love turns fear out of doors *and* expels every trace of terror! For fear brings with it the thought of punishment, and [so] he who is afraid has not reached the full maturity of love [is not yet grown into love's complete perfection]". This is one of many reasons the Holy Spirit desires to empower you with a fresh, double anointing that will quicken your growth, shape your will, heal your emotions, and deliver you from the spirit of fear.

Moreover, listen to the apostle Paul's solemn warning in 1 Thessalonians 5:2 regarding the looming times that are rapidly approaching the human race. "For you yourselves know perfectly well that the day of the [return of the] Lord will come [as unexpectedly and suddenly] as a thief in the night." On one hand, that day has nothing to do with the Church. It takes place during the Great Tribulation, before the second phase of Jesus's second coming, the Revelation, or the appearing of Christ. But on the other hand, the Church needs to work diligently and faithfully to help prepare the unprepared for the Rapture that takes place before the Great Tribulation, followed by the second phase of Christ's second coming seven years later. Know and cherish today as a new, one-time opportunity of unmerited and unearned grace. Proclaim the righteousness of God; share the good news of the gospel of Jesus Christ.

Use this book, *Forgetting, Remembering, Reaching*, as an instrument to encourage everyone within your sphere of influence. Emphasize the importance of living life in the now presence and will of God. It is my prayer that you, by faith, understand that God's abundant blessings for you are much greater than anything you can ask, think, or imagine. It is also my heart's desire that this book will take you closer to that reality.

Chapter 1

What If?

What if life were begun at the tomb and ended in the womb? What if you knew every detail of your life from the beginning and understood that every decision made in this life will be judged after this life? Chances are, you would not do many of the things you have done or are doing. Moreover, the temptation to postpone, ignore, or reject trusting God wholeheartedly would be far less tempting, if not avoided altogether. However, an answer to these what if questions is less important than the soul-searching journey that they will likely take you on. The what if questions should remind the believer of the consequences of sin and rebellion, and prayerfully lead the unbeliever to accept Christ as Lord and Savior. But if you are already saved, your obvious choice should be to know Christ more intimately.

Regardless of your answers to the questions, please remember the Word of God is forever settled in the Heavens. So whether you accept or reject the commandments and precepts of God, they are still forever settled, and also the penalty for sin is forever settled in the Word of God: "For the wages which sin pays is death, but the [bountiful] free gift of God is eternal life through (in union with) Jesus Christ our Lord" (Rom. 6:23).

The questions were asked to inspire you to cherish life, to warn the young not to rush their years, and to encourage the elderly not to dread their passing. If you, for example, ask a young child his or her age, the answer will usually echo, for example, a sense of pride and joy, "I'm seven going on eight," when it is common knowledge that eight is the next number after seven. On the other hand, some adults seem less willing to tell their age. But regardless of your age, each of us is older today than we have ever been and as young as we will ever be. In other words, none of us is younger today than we were yesterday.

While a young child may anxiously and expectantly look forward to the next birthday, to some adults it serves as an uneasy reminder, a tap on the shoulder, as that of an unwanted timekeeper's warning that time is running out of the time. Each year, especially the latter ones, is a stern reminder that far less time remains. Children, from their innocent and untested points of view, are convinced they can master life. Adults who reflect over the years are sometimes ashamed that more was not done, that waiting to do tomorrow what should have been done today was an unwise decision with undesirable consequences that cannot be overturned or reversed.

The truth to glean from these facts is that the passing of time is beyond our control. While children will not necessarily master time, they may believe adults have failed miserably to master it. Regardless of your point of view, this is a solemn warning that life is a precious gift that should be lived with a divine sense of urgency. Furthermore, it remains to be seen whether the present generation of youth will live longer than the generations before them, but the elderly have certainly lived longer than the young have at this present time. Therefore, neither the young nor the old has any bragging rights. However, when the young and the aged, the visionaries and the dreamers, work together to spread the gospel of Jesus Christ, we become a powerful army against the works of the devil. This book, *Forgetting, Remembering, Reaching*, will help adults remember to do what children are prayerfully learning to do – love, trust, forget, and forgive.

Think on These Things

As you think on or rethink the *hypothetical* questions asked earlier, add these to the list: Would I be a better person if I knew exactly how old I will live to be, or when the Rapture will take place? And if I knew the exact date and hour that my life would end in this life, or when Christ would rapture the church, would I serve God more faithfully? Or, if I already know what I should be doing, how can I become more committed to doing it?

Whether or not you choose to think on these things is, of course, a matter of choice. But what if God told you that you would die or that Jesus would rapture the Church in exactly thirty days? While it is obvious that no such warning will be given, for the sake of what if, how would you spend your precious month? This question and the others are super hypothetical, to say the least, but your answers to them are not. While you may be thinking about how or why you should answer them, please allow me to share how I believe I would use my thirty days.

If it were a case of me dying, after I finished asking God why me, I would carefully examine my relationship with Him. If there were known sins in my life, I would immediately repent and commit not to commit them anymore. Since I am married, I would lovingly and thoughtfully communicate with my wife in a very tender and attentive way. I would enjoy our time together, as if it were our first date, and enjoy our last month together by showering her with all my love and affection. I would lovingly hug our children. Moreover, devote time to doing the things they enjoy without allowing our age difference to make a difference. I would do my best to answer all their questions that may have previously seemed childish and unimportant. Also, I would tell everyone I talked with, whether loved ones, friends, strangers, or the not-so-friendly, that I love them. I would let everyone know that his or her life adds meaning to mine. I would unselfishly share the gifts, abilities, talents, and resources God has blessed me with. I would also share the joyous gift of life and the unfailing power of love.

The point being, whatever you or I would do is exactly what we should be doing all the time. So don't wait until it's too late to obey the voice of God. Today is the time to share the message that love is the reason God sacrificed His only Son. Moreover, always remember you were created from love, redeemed from sin by love, and commanded to share with others the good news with love and kindness.

"For God so greatly loved *and* dearly prized the world that He [even] gave up His only begotten (unique) Son, so that whoever believes in (trusts in, clings to, relies on) Him shall not perish (come to destruction, be lost) but have eternal (everlasting) life" (John 3:16) is the explicit expression of God's love. And in I John 4:7 we are told, "Beloved, let us love one another, for love is (springs) from God; and he who loves [his fellowmen] is begotten (born) of God and is coming [progressively] to know *and* understand God [to perceive and recognize and get a better and clearer knowledge of Him"]. It is God's command for believers to love one another. Since God is the purest and holiest expression of love, use the previous questions to count the cost of redemption and commit to embracing the precious gift of life!

God Knows

Whenever God asks us questions, it is a *no-brainer* that He already knows the answers. For example, God asked Adam in Genesis 3:11a, "Who told you that you were naked?" He asked Adam to allow him to admit what he had done, repent, and accept the consequences and punishment for his disobedience. Because of Adam's fall, God offers forgiveness and salvation through His Son Jesus Christ. Therefore, it is the duty of the redeemed to share His love in the power of the Holy Spirit by introducing the lost to the Savior. Yet, before you can become the person God created you to be, you must first crucify the innate nature of sin and rebellion and allow the Spirit of Christ to transform you into His likeness. This uncompromising process necessarily involves forgetting the past, remembering the gift of salvation, and reaching for the recreated life of God for the redeemed.

Toward this end, we can learn a lot about the power of love and forgiveness from children who will quickly let go of hurt and disappointment. Unless influenced by uncaring and unforgiving parents or adults, children's short-lived disagreements and childish spats perfectly exemplify the dynamics of *forgetting, remembering, and reaching.*

Since God's grace cannot be earned, the forgiven must be willing to forgive. In other words, the forgiving person is also forgiven! To walk in a spirit of forgiveness, ask yourself, "Who and whose am I?" But think before you answer, because faith demands a truthful answer to a simple, yet profound question. If the question is ignored or not answered, it may become a thorn rooted in the depths of your soul, and your spiritual growth will definitely suffer.

Chapter 2

Born In Captivity

The tragedy of a person not knowing his or her true identity was made very clear during a circus performance. The female lion tamer, armed with only a whip and a long prod, masterfully controlled the five lions within the small cage. Several of the beasts sat sluggishly by, obediently awaiting their turn to perform while the onlookers sat nervously on the edges of their seats. The faint and hovering stink of beast and the oohs and aahs from the crowd created a tensed atmosphere in the lofty, dome-shaped coliseum where demonstrators were once arrested and corralled into close quarters like livestock at an auction.

Whether the act involved one, two, or all five lions, the beasts obeyed her gentle voice. With the crack of the whip, they stood upright on hind legs, jumped through rings of fire, showing their long and sharp teeth as they roared and clawed at the lion tamer. Amid a breathtaking performance, the French beauty turned away from the flesh-eating, roaring beasts and bowed gracefully to the cheering and awestruck crowd as the lions roared and pawed in the background.

It was an amazing yet saddening scene that a petite woman in a small cage was controlling five magnificent animals, feared and respected in the jungle by man and the animal kingdom. What if a lion from the jungle were watching this spectacle? Surely it would not have understood how such a small and fragile creature was able to control such power and might! Nonetheless, more than five thousand cheering and captivated spectators sat on the edge of their seats, seemingly praying the beautiful lion tamer would not be killed or maimed, yet fascinated by the possibility that she might. While the crowd saw the lions as wild and dangerous beasts, to the tamer they were adorable animals trained to entertain and mesmerize audiences.

In the wild, the lion rules as king of the jungle. But these magnificent beasts, born or trained in captivity, knew nothing of their beastly ability to hunt and to rule. Lions by nature, they had never chased zebras across the plains of Africa. As the undisputed king of the jungle, they had never used their keen sense of smell to stalk and kill their prey. As the ruler of the jungle, they had never instilled fear throughout the jungle with a ferocious roar and their stalking presence. Although the circus spectators recognized them as lions, they did not know they were lions, the undisputed king of the jungle, created by God to roam and rule the wild. Instead, they were born in captivity, or either trained in an environment that suppressed their true nature, repressed their animalistic instincts, and deprived them of living in the jungle as a lion's lion!

What's Your Captivity?

Like those lions, we too were born in captivity. The disobedience of Adam and Eve is responsible for every human being, without exception, being born in captivity. Regardless of your family tree, race, birthplace, or financial status, you were born in a fallen state that is the result of being born, from a spiritual perspective, on death row, separated from the love of God and the God of love. But unlike the lions, helplessly trapped in bondage for circus amusement, Jesus is waiting at the door of every captive's heart to set him or her free. Although you did not personally choose to be born into sin bondage, it is by choice whether or not you are set free from it. Only in Christ are you more than a conqueror! But if Satan is allowed to use his whip or prod tricks to control your mind and steal your inheritance, you will remain the victim of sin captivity in this world and will not become the person God created you to be from the beginning. The lion by birthright is king of the jungle. You, by rebirth, are more than a conqueror in Christ Jesus.

Nevertheless, Satan has been plotting before and since your spiritual birth to keep you in bondage. Unless you learn to walk in victory, he may succeed by convincing you that he is the conqueror. Even though he is brazenly masked with a stinging whip, nudging prod, camouflaged lies, and enticing deception, do not accept anything he says or does. God sent His Son into this world to set you free, and Jesus sent the Holy Spirit to teach you how to remain free. The total of our freedom is shared by Jesus in John 8:36 – "So if the Son liberates you [makes you free men], then you are really and unquestionably free." Yet this truth is much deeper than having intellectual knowledge of the Bible and Jesus' teachings. The Holy Spirit's indwelling presence empowers the believer to walk in his or her deliverance, secured by Christ's sacrifice on the cross.

However, in that each of us is born in a state of captivity that separates us from God, salvation is the only way to be liberated. The sooner we accept Christ as Lord and Savior, the sooner we are delivered from captivity. When Jesus is received as Lord and Savior, the Word cleanses the mind, soul, and body from a lifetime of sin bondage and carnal thinking, and life is henceforward lived in the power of God's might. To attain this realm of deliverance and authority in Christ, it is vitally important to recognize the underlying source of bondage. Proverbs. 23:7a states, "For as he thinks in his heart, so is he." As long as the mind is imprisoned by the lies of Satan, that person will remain in bondage because the mind is in bondage. On the other hand, the process of learning to think like Christ thinks necessarily means the thoughts and ways of Christ replace our thoughts and ways.

Therefore, this book, *Forgetting, Remembering, Reaching*, will help every committed and earnest believer to crucify the old man with the mind of Christ. The transformation process requires forgetting worldly things, remembering and reaching for the promises of God with diligent and uncompromising commitment.

The Art of *Forgetting, Remembering, and Reaching*

In Genesis 18:10-14, God reveals His plan for Abraham and Sarah to have a child. ["The Lord] said, I will surely return to you when the season comes round, and behold, Sarah your wife will have a son. And Sarah was listening and heard it at the tent door, which was behind Him. [Compare Rom. 9:9-12.] Now Abraham and Sarah were old, well advanced in years; it had ceased to be with Sarah as with [young] women. [She was past the age of childbearing]. Therefore Sarah laughed to herself, saying, After I have become aged shall I have pleasure and delight, my lord (husband), being old also?" [Compare I Pet. 3:6.] And the Lord asked Abraham, Why did Sarah laugh, saying, Shall I really bear a child when I am so old? Is anything too hard or too wonderful for the Lord? At the appointed time, when the season [for her delivery] comes around, I will return to you and Sarah shall have borne a son" [Compare Matt. 19:26.] It was understandable that Sarah secretly laughed when she overheard the Lord's promise.

It is also understandable that human logic and common sense gave her reason to doubt God. She was not only past childbearing age, but also her desire for sexual intimacy had dwindled to an occasional faint memory. Yet God promised them a son, and to remove all doubt from their minds, an angel of the Lord asked Abraham a rhetorical question of profound importance in Genesis 18:14a that is also for you and me. "Is anything too hard *or* too wonderful for the Lord?" He then reaffirms the promise by assuring him that *at the appointed time,* he would return, quicken Sarah's aged body, and she would conceive the promised child, Isaac.

It is later revealed that Abraham believed what God had said, and his faith was credited to him as righteousness. But before he and Sarah could believe God for the child, they had to forget about their age and everything else that said having a child was impossible. To forget about their age, they, despite overwhelming odds, remembered the promise that in due season or "at the appointed time," a child would be born. By remembering God's promise, they were able to reach the faith realm and receive it.

Moreover, Isaiah 55:7 unveils several profound truths that ensure victory for the faithful heirs of Abraham's blessings. "Let the wicked forsake his way and the unrighteous man his thoughts; and let him return to the Lord, and He will have love, pity, and mercy for him, and to our God, for He will multiply to him His abundant pardon." An unrighteous person's thoughts will produce a wicked lifestyle. In other words, unrighteous thoughts always pave the way for sinful actions and unwanted consequences. In verse 8, God reveals, "For My thoughts are not your thoughts, neither are your ways My ways, says the Lord." The reason our ways are not God's ways is that our thoughts are not His thoughts. In verse 9, God says His ways and thoughts, and our thoughts and ways are as far apart as heaven and earth. "For as the heavens are higher than the earth, so are My ways higher than your ways and My thoughts than your thoughts."

The most effective and decisive way of forgetting is to live in the present with your eyes steadfastly fixed on the mark of the high calling of God in Christ Jesus! By living in the now, you will not dwell on the past or worry about the future. Living in the now unseats unfruitful memories of the past and empowers you to prepare for the future that arrives one thought and one decision at a time from over time.

When you live life in the now, you will learn how to deal with people lovingly and practically. You will also deal with trials and tribulations without looking at them through the eyes of fear and doubt. When you deal with people you know as if you just met them, and strangers as if you have always known them, you will be able to see everyone through the eyes of God. Commit to dealing with people lovingly and fairly. Do not be unfairly critical of their past nor prejudge their future. Refuse to imagine, retain, summon, or interject negative memories into the present that appear to be a repeat of the past. Forgetting empowers you to face today with a caring and loving heart. Love sees beyond the surface through the eyes of grace, mercy, and forgivingness.

Escape the Wilderness Captivity

If you choose to live in sin and disobedience, it will become your residence of choice. The children of Israel, for example, prayed for a deliverer for four hundred years. God sent Moses to Egypt to deliver them out of bondage, but they willfully and repeatedly rebelled against God's anointed one. The

Bible records a sad commentary that they wandered in the wilderness for forty years! The mighty hand of God was upon Moses to lead them from Egypt to Canaan, but their affection for Egypt caused them to yearn for the place of bondage that they had prayed to be delivered from. The complainers wandered in the wilderness for forty years, and perished.

As you can see, it is possible to pray without necessarily desiring or earnestly expecting to receive an answer. Hypocritically, one can develop a ritualistic prayer life while courting a warped kind of love for bondage and suffering. If this happens, the act, not an answer, becomes the object or reason for prayer. Therefore, be sure you desire what you are praying for and are expecting an answer from God. Also, faith–empowered prayer must be faithfully acted upon with decisive actions. Otherwise, there is a real danger of becoming comfortable in the wilderness of sin and disobedience.

Chapter 3

Forgetting Takes Courage and Obedience

The apostle Paul addresses several important issues in his epistle to the church in Philippi. We can take what he said to the Philippian saints and apply it to our lives. Throughout his letter, the saints were charged to know that we are children of the Most High God, and were encouraged to press forward by forgetting and reaching. What Paul said is an important part of this book; therefore, selective scriptures are included to help us to clearly understand that it is our reasonable service to also fulfill our calling.

Although several precious lessons are revealed in his epistle, an urgent warning was and is the dangers of pride and self-inflicted egos, which Paul addresses by sharing a brief and personal history of his life as Saul of Tarsus. He was an educated Pharisee from a prestigious bloodline, and although very zealous, his misgivings about Christ misled him into persecuting the church. However, everything changed when he had a life-changing encounter with the risen Christ on the road to Damascus. The encounter not only changed the course of his life, but his contributions to the Church are second only to Jesus Christ Himself.

Unlike Paul, a zealous Pharisee who became an apostle, some of us who were the life of the party before we were saved tend to fade quietly into the background after accepting Christ as our Savior. Then, sadly, do next to nothing to spread the gospel of Jesus Christ. If you were a go-getter sinner, be a go-getter saint! Don't stop doing. Change what and whom you are doing it with and for! If you were a dedicated sinner, commit to being a committed saint.

Take a closer look at Paul's impressive lineage and accomplishments. It is easy to recognize that none of his achievements won him any brownie points with God. Please do not forget to remember that God is not and cannot be impressed with the things that impress us. Furthermore, God qualifies the unqualified, teaches the untaught, and trains the untrained.

A closer look at the life of Paul deserves our attention.

Worthless Bragging Rights

The rise of false teachers was and remains a threat to the Church. They continue to contaminate the holiness of God to stifle personal growth, silence the gospel, and deceive the body of Christ by parading family background, education, and success as bragging rights. Paul counters their deception in Philippians 3:1-6 by sharing his impressive achievements that he admits are worthless. "FOR THE rest, my brethren, delight yourselves in the Lord and continue to rejoice that you are in Him. To keep writing to you [over and over] of the same things is not irksome to me, and it is [a precaution] for your safety. Look out for those dogs [Judaizers, legalists], look out for those mischief-makers, look out for those who mutilate the flesh. For we [Christians] are the true circumcision, who worship God in spirit and by the Spirit of God and exult and glory and pride ourselves in Jesus Christ, and put no confidence or dependence [on what we are] in the flesh and on our outward privileges and physical advantages and external appearances–Though for myself I have [at least grounds] to rely on the flesh. If any other man considers that he has or seems to have reason to rely on the flesh and his physical and outward advantages, I have still more! Circumcised when I was eight days old, of the race of Israel, of the tribe of Benjamin, a Hebrew [and the son] of Hebrews; as to the observance of the Law I was of [the party of] the Pharisees. As to my zeal, I was a persecutor of the church, and by the Law's standard of righteousness (supposed justice, uprightness, and right standing with God) I was proven to be blameless and no fault was found with me."

Despite his bloodline and impressive credentials, their spiritual value was worthless, even though he was born into an affluent family, received the very best education, and enjoyed a remarkable career. Moreover, he admitted that persecuting the church was, according to the Law, nothing but the zealous pursuit of a futile goal that he committed to out of spiritual ignorance. From his credentials as a Pharisee, he was both respected and envied, but his personal, historical, and sinful ignorance had misguided him into wronging both himself and Christ. It was only after Saul met Jesus on the road to Damascus that he realized neither fame nor fortune was worthy to be compared with his new life in Christ.

Thus, his former successes, now viewed as failures or dung, were shared as a warning to false teachers and believers in Philippi. His message also echoes a stern warning for us: if anyone had a right to brag, based on accomplishments, Paul was all the more qualified. But when he compared his life to Christ's, his bragging rights and self-image were immediately reduced to rubbish and thrown out the time-honored window of his past religious beliefs.

However, God can make something precious from seemingly nothing. Jesus used Paul's personal and professional experiences, as He does all of ours, to undergird his ministry, to refocus his devotion to transform his life, and to bless the body of Christ through him. Paul's message in Philippians 3:13 continues to change lives. "I do not consider, brethren, that I have captured and made it my own [yet]; but one thing I do [it is my one aspiration]: forgetting what lies behind and straining forward to what lies ahead."

Back to Forgetting

The substance of our thoughts and their impact on history are very important. Also, what, when, why, and how something is remembered influences our decisions and helps to control the desires of the heart, past, present, and future. The apostle Paul says in 2 Corinthians 4:18, "Since we consider and look not to the things that are seen but to the things that are unseen; for the things that are visible are temporal (brief and fleeting), but the things that are invisible are deathless and everlasting."

Do not become so obsessed with your needs that you neglect to face painful and unwelcome experiences of the past. Do not fail to seek eternal growth and spiritual maturity. Remember, the body you are now living in is not your permanent home. It will be changed in the resurrection; this mortal will put on immortality, and this corruption shall put on incorruption. The mortal body is slowly perishing in the interim between the temporal and the eternal. Imagine the perishing of the physical body as that of a block of ice melting in the sunlight that changes its form, but not its substance. On the other hand, while the body grows weaker and older each day, the inner or spirit man is growing stronger and abounding in the strength of Jesus Christ.

If what you are looking at or thinking about is visible or a lingering and unfruitful memory, it is a passing passion of the mind. Even though this may be challenging to accept, the believer is instructed to look at, through the eyes of faith, the spiritual things that are invisible to the natural eye. How, you may ask? The promises of God, many of which you cannot see, touch, smell, taste, or hear amid the noise and haste in the physical realm, are eternal and universal in scope. Therefore, allow the Spirit of Christ to reveal to you, through and in the Word, the glory of God. In the meantime, do not allow the mind to apply carnal reasoning to spiritual promises and realities.

If you allow your natural mind to romance cherished memories, you are in grave danger of becoming obsessed with the past. If you ignore the present, you may find yourself lusting for the future, instead of living in the NOW presence of God. As if sleepwalking in a fantasy world, this sort of folly taints the present and creates unrealistic expectations for the future, intermingled with misleading memories from the past. It is therefore an inborn danger to waste valuable time and precious energy thinking about past desires and regrets, or imagining future fears and dreams. If the need to forget is consistently ignored, the past will constantly haunt you, and may destroy opportunities to live in the NOW. This will cause the present to become a source of constant fear, and hope for the future dwindles to an uncertain possibility. It is unfruitful to spend time trying to relive or unlive the past. Commit to possessing the promises of God that are now yours.

When I first began studying Philippians 3:13, it seemed odd that Paul did not mention the present. Instead, his focus was on the past and the future, forgetting and reaching. But after several months, the Holy Spirit revealed to me why the present was treated as if it did not exist. The arrival and departure of the present is, in a sense, an inseparable process. Its beginning and ending take place within the same passing moment. For this reason the believer is to follow the example of Paul, "I press on toward the goal to win the [supreme and heavenly] prize to which God in Christ Jesus is calling us upward" (Phil. 3:14). If this verse is ignored or put on the back burner, one's affection and commitment to God can quickly be disrupted by the out–of–reach past. Moreover, the present and the unborn future are being delivered from the womb of time that always arrives and departs in the passing present.

Since the past cannot be relived and the present cannot be prolonged, it is the future that gives balance to time and our relationship to, in, and with it. Imagine time, the past, present, and the future as that of driving on an unfamiliar interstate at seventy miles per hour. The vehicle is constantly moving from where it temporarily was to where it temporarily is. Yet, in a sense of speaking, it is not in any one place long enough to say that it is in any one particular place. Again, think about an interstate that you are traveling on, trying to find your way, and just ahead are lots of signs with arrows pointing in different directions. You are unsure of which exit to take or what sign to read and follow. As soon as you are close enough to read the signs, you have passed them. As long as you were driving toward the signs, you were, in a sense of speaking, reaching for them, but they were part of the present no longer than that split second it took you to pass them. Once you have passed the signs, a glance in the rearview mirror reveals there are no directions on their backsides, making looking back a dangerous waste of time.

So, not forgetting and reaching is dangerous and the forfeiture of divine opportunities. However, forgetting frees you from where, who, and what you were, and reaching takes you to where you are going and prepares you to be the person you are becoming. Therefore, allow yourself to grow stronger and responsibly, but do not try to prolong or rush the growth process. If you are forgetting and reaching, the short-lived present will serve its purpose to lead you continuously forward into the future.

The key to growth and maturity is to always obey the Word of God. This is the reason the believer is instructed in the Bible to be both a hearer who becomes a doer of the Word. It is therefore action and not idleness that turns a hearer into a doer. In James 1:23–24 the Word clearly states, "For if anyone only listens to the Word without obeying it and being a doer of it, he is like a man who looks carefully at his [own] natural face in a mirror; For he thoughtfully observes himself, and then goes off and promptly forgets what he was like."

For just a moment, think about the purpose of a mirror. It allows you to see a reflection of yourself, but it cannot change what you see or who you are. As soon as you walk away, what you saw quickly fades into a faint and unclear memory. But the Word is the mirror of God that manifests an inner reflection of who we are in Him. The Word of God allows us to see ourselves as we focus on, and remain in focus or attuned with the will of God. The Word helps us to identify strengths and weaknesses. It empowers the believer to build on the righteousness of God and to eliminate every surrendered area of unrighteousness. Unless faithfully devoted to God and His righteousness, life will remain or become unclear, unfulfilled, undirected, and misdirected.

The past can also be likened to a role of used film. Each exposure is a fond memory of an experience that is now nothing more than that, a fond memory. The photos may rekindle a desire to relive the experience, but they are only snapshots of the past, not a realistic picture of the present or the future. Old pictures and yearning memories are nostalgic and cherished possessions. Nevertheless, resist longing or daydreaming about reliving the past. If committed to experiencing peace and victory in this life, give the past its proper due, bury and retire it. Do not allow the past to get in the way of the present and delay or deter the possibilities for the future.

Forgetting is Not the Inability to Remember

Forgetting is not the same as not remembering. It is a carefully reached decision to remember past experiences healthily and realistically. The following example and scriptures are not only about forgetting and remembering, but they also illustrate the importance of remembering how to let go of, forget, and release the past to the past. However, remembering what should have been forgotten or forgetting what should have been remembered is equally bad.

Take Peter, for example. He made a hasty promise driven by conflicting and erratic emotions that prevented him from realizing the seriousness of his promise. Consequently, he did the very thing he had vowed not to do. He was offended and denied Jesus. Peter either denied Jesus because he feared for his safety if he admitted he knew Him, or he forgot to remember his promise. Here's how the conversation went. "Peter declared to Him, Though they all are offended *and* stumble *and* fall away because of You [and distrust and desert You], **I** will never do so. Jesus said to him, Solemnly **I** declare to you, this very night, before a single rooster crows, you will deny *and* disown **Me** three times. Peter said to Him, Even if **I** must die with **You**, **I** will not deny *or* disown **You**! And all the disciples said the same thing" (Matt. 26:33-35).

Let us fast forward to Jesus's arrest, crucifixion, and the events that occurred after His resurrection. Jesus stood on the shore and told Peter where to cast his net to catch fish, and when Peter and the disciples came ashore, "Jesus came and took the bread and gave it to them, and so also [with] the fish. This was now the third time that Jesus revealed Himself (appeared, was manifest) to the disciples after He had risen from the dead. When they had eaten, Jesus said to Simon Peter, Simon, son of John, do you love Me more than these [others do–with reasoning, intentional, spiritual devotion, as one loves the Father]? He said to Him, Yes, Lord, You know that I love You [that I have deep, instinctive, personal affection for You, as for a close friend]. He said to him, Feed My lambs. Again He said to him the second time, Simon, son of John, do you love Me [with reasoning, intentional, spiritual devotion, as one loves the Father]? He said to Him, Yes, Lord, You know that I love You [that I have a deep, instinctive, personal affection for You, as for a close friend]. He said to him, Shepherd (tend) My sheep. He said to him the third time, Simon, son of John, do you love Me [with a deep, instinctive, personal affection for Me, as for a close friend]? Peter was grieved (was saddened and was hurt) that He should ask him the third time, Do you love Me? And he said to Him, Lord, You know everything; You know that I love You [that I have a deep, instinctive, personal affection for You, as for a close friend]. Jesus said to him, Feed My sheep" (John 21:13-17).

Jesus was asking Peter if his love for Him was like that of a Father, and Peter confessed his love for Jesus was as that of a close friend. Jesus was referring to agape love, but Peter was expressing phileo love. Jesus's reason for asking Peter the same question three times, addressing him by his full name most of the time, is very important. He wanted Peter to gain a deeper understanding of love, and rightfully so. The word love is so widely used and misused that its true meaning is often lost in conversation. But before I continue the discussion about love between Jesus and Peter, please allow me to warn you: When you talk about love with someone you love, make very sure the two of you are speaking the same love language. Let us now return to Jesus and Peter. The first two times Jesus questioned Peter, He was referring to agape love, a true and unselfish devotion to the one loved. But since Peter responded to Jesus with phileo love or brotherly kindness, Jesus asked him the third time with phileo love in mind because that is the only love Peter was capable of sharing at the time.

Jesus also questioned Peter three times to introduce him to the three-phased commission to feed His lambs and sheep. As important as these facts are, they also stress the importance of forgetting and remembering, and they serve as a reminder that forgetting is not a clinical matter of erasing from memory previous events or experiences. Forgetting is remembering without harboring hateful and revengeful thoughts or unresolved memories. Jesus also asked Peter the same question three times because He had denied them three times. On one hand, Jesus wanted Peter to clearly understand what He was telling him to do. On the other hand, Jesus was reminding Peter, not to punish him but to encourage him that his past would not prevent him from his commission to feed His lambs and sheep.

We too can learn to love people and ourselves with the same agape love and forgiveness Jesus granted Peter. When you remember past events, use them to build and not to destroy, to encourage and not to discourage, to edify and not to tear down. Therefore, forgetting is a matter of remembering the past in such a way that memories are used to help everyone involved to fulfill their calling. Learn not to use unpleasant memories and undesirable experiences as a stumbling block that will hinder growth and maturity. Negative memories that are being remembered to inflict hurt and pain have no place in the present affairs of your life.

Chapter 4

Just Believe!

The Word of God is forever settled: "Jesus said to her, did I not tell you and promise you that if you would believe and rely on Me, you would see the glory of God?" (John 11:40.) Regardless of trials and tribulations, even to the point of death, trust God and you will see the glory or the manifestation of His power working on your behalf. Irrespective of the situations or circumstances, deliverance is made manifest when belief is nourished with faith in God, energized with a heartfelt and heart-knowing confession not swayed by feelings or conditions. Unwavering faith stands firmly on the promises of God, even when facing serious opposition or uncertainties, whether it takes a day or much longer for deliverance to manifest. Always remember the Word of God is the transport of faith. It empowers and extends hope beyond its natural limits into the supernatural realm, where the unfruitful becomes fruitful and the impossible becomes possible. Faith creates an atmosphere of unwavering expectations for God to bless you, even if it involves Him creating an unparalleled miracle especially for you.

Shadrach, Meshach, and Abednego are an archetypical or classic example of faith and God's faithfulness. King Nebuchadnezzar gave them the choice of worshipping his golden image or they would be tossed into the fiery furnace. Of all the condemned people that had been tossed into the fiery furnace, not a single person had ever been rescued or removed from it alive. Yet when given the demand to either worship Nebuchadnezzar's false god or be tossed into the furnace, the three young men boldly and faithfully proclaimed, "If our God Whom we serve is able to deliver us from the burning fiery furnace, He will deliver us out of your hand, O king" (Dan. 3:17). Some translations interpret this verse slightly differently, but these young men said in essence, whether thrown in the fiery furnace or not, they would not yield to his decree and serve the image. Furthermore, they said God would deliver them, and God delivered them from a horrible death chamber that not a single person had ever survived!

Although the entire Bible is a complete revelation of the sovereign God, Shadrach, Meshach, and Abednego trusted the faithfulness of God at a time when they did not have the entire Bible to embolden or support their trust and faith in Him. Moreover, fire, unless controlled and used for the good of humanity, is a destructive force capable of destroying both property and all manner of life. Nonetheless, these patriarchs did not deny Jesus, but they ardently refused to worship the golden image. They not only refused, they said, "But if not, let it be known to you, O king, that we will not serve your gods, or worship the golden image which you have set up!"—(Dan. 3:18). In other words, their decision was final, regardless of what the king did. Whether he put them in the furnace or not, they refused to serve the golden image. What an expression of faith!

Unfortunately, however, the preceding verse is often interpreted or misinterpreted to mean God can save, whether He does or not. And that's true. But they had already confessed God would deliver them, so why would they do an about-face and doubt what they just said He would do? However, if you believe it is possible to have too much faith in God, I submit to you that anyone who says He's able even if He doesn't has too little faith in God. God saved the patriarchs of faith who were standing on the Word, obeying His will because they expected and deserved nothing less of Him. In any event, the furnace was heated to a temperature hotter than it had ever been, but when Christ showed up in the fiery furnace, the young men of faith were unaffected by it.

Another testimony of faithfulness is that of Noah, who had no idea what rain was; yet he built the ark because God told him it was going to rain. Too, God delivered Moses and the children of Israel at the Red Sea, and Daniel in the lion's den. In each situation, faith was not based on God having performed any similar miracles. But these patriarchs were operating in God's divine will, and they knew and trusted Him because He is God, and they knew there is none other like Him. On the other hand, you and I have the entire Bible. It not only reveals God's supreme and creative ability to do the impossible, but the Bible also teaches us He is willing to provide for us whatever is needed, whenever and wherever it is needed!

Keep in mind, however, that these patriarchs of faith were delivered from certain danger by forgetting temporal circumstances, remembering the promises of God, and reaching for His eternal glory. Previous defeats, cowardliness, or the faithlessness of others were not used as an excuse for them to doubt God. All their negative thoughts and experiences, if there were any, were forgotten and pushed aside by remembering the omnipotent God, they reached into the realm of faith, where the supernatural rules the natural and transforms the natural into the supernatural.

After all, faith is the spiritual substance that empowers and sustains the believer. It is therefore impossible to walk in victory or to please God without faith. For it is written in Hebrews 11:6, "But without faith it is impossible to please and be satisfactory to Him. For whoever would come near to God must [necessarily] believe that God exists and that He is the rewarder of those who earnestly and diligently seek Him [out]." The word diligently exemplifies unstoppable faith. Also, each of us is given the measure of faith that is not given to us by wishful thinking from the sidelines of doubt, disbelief, or unbelief. Faith is much more than a subtle belief system. It is equal to righteousness itself.

In Romans 4:22 the apostle Paul writes "That is why his faith was credited to him as righteousness (right standing with God") as he reflects on Genesis 15:6, "And he [Abram] believed in (trusted in, relied on, remained steadfast to) the Lord, and He counted it to him as righteousness (right standing with God)." These two verses connect an inseparable bond between faith and righteousness. Faith and unrighteousness or unbelief and righteousness do not agree, and they therefore cannot walk together because they are contrary to each other and unlike God. On the other hand, it is impossible to please God if faith is watered down with up-and-down doubts of ifs, ands, and buts. You will end up living in and out of fellowship with God.

The root of spiritual growth is faith, and its source is the Word. It takes faith to become the person God created you to be. According to II Corinthians 5:17, the spiritual transformation begins with salvation and continues throughout one's entire life. "Therefore if any person is [ingrafted] in Christ (the Messiah) he is a new creation (a new creature altogether); the old [previous moral and spiritual condition] has passed away. Behold, the fresh and new has come!" A deeper level of faith is possible and essential for the diligent seeker to be changed from faith to faith into the likeness of Christ. While the transformation process involves growth, live each day as the first day of new growth, grace, and mercy. Seek to become the person God created you to be.

Spiritually speaking, this is made possible by God's grace, but continual growth comes from a steadfast willingness to let go of the past by *forgetting, remembering, and reaching.* Think of the process as awakening in the morning, refreshed and reinvigorated, as undeniable proof of having slept. Although you will not be able to pinpoint the exact time you fell asleep, the fact that you are waking up, alert and energetic, is proof that you have been asleep. Think of forgetting as releasing the things of the past, remembering the present, and reaching as embracing the future.

You may or may not be aware of every growth step along the way, but you will awake one morning from a growth-stunting stupor and realize you are dawning on the horizon of a spiritual breakthrough. You will know you have grown from where you were, but be careful not to allow your mind to wander in the broad and the wide, and miss the strait and narrow gate that leads to life.

Chapter 5

The Battle For Your Mind

The mind is a thought factory constantly working on different concepts and ideas at all times, at the same time. The day shift, if you will, works most effectively when focused on what you are doing. The night shift works from a subconscious or unconscious level, especially when you are asleep, or when the mind is adrift in the sea of uncharted waters, thinking and reasoning without purpose or direction. Much of the time, the night shift also deals with matters that were not resolved or ignored by the mind on the dayshift. So, it is not a matter of whether or not the thought factory is at work, but it is a matter of identifying the thoughts it is working on or avoiding.

In that the mind is a thought factory, it is important to take authority over what you think and are reproducing in it. Regardless of what is going on around us, the battle is won or lost in the mind before it is fought on the battlefield of life. Nonetheless, every believer is a child of God; you can be victorious over the enemy through Christ Jesus. Moreover, the Bible reveals Satan is a defeated foe, and we have overcome him through the greater One who lives in us. The war was settled more than two thousand years ago at Calvary, and there is not the slightest possibility that Satan can do anything to overthrow the victory that is forever settled in the Heavens. However, it is possible for Satan, though he has already lost the war, to attack individual believers who, if not watchful, may lose a battle or scrimmage to him. Still, Christ won the war at Calvary. The war is won. Satan is defeated. Guard against losing battles to the enemy, though he is working hellishly hard to contaminate your mind with lies and deception.

For this reason, the diligent believer must understand the nature of the battlefield in which Satan spreads lies and uses warlike tactics against the body of Christ. His ploys, though meant to frustrate you, are not so much a matter of what he can do, but what you allow him, for whatever reason(s), to do.

The devil is cunning, and he uses whatever we allow him to use against us. Remember, what the mind accepts, the body believes and obeys.

The mind is therefore under constant attack by enemies from within, much more than it is from outside forces. Sometimes the enemies of the mind are spiritual, and at other times they are mental, psychological, physical, emotional, physiological, or some other harassing type of fear. It is for these reasons that *forgetting, remembering, and reaching* are so vitally important. To recognize and walk in Christ's victory, inflicted on Satan at Calvary, whose strategy is to capture, captivate, and conquer the mind, you must force him out of hiding into the spiritual realm of truth and righteousness. When you do, he cannot threaten you with sins of commission or omission that you have confessed and repented of.

Thus, forgetting and repenting work together. Also, forgetting involves forgiving yourself for what you did or did not do. Focus on remembering who you are. Reaching within awakens the person you are becoming is a necessary but challenging step in the process. In other words, we must remember and acknowledge what we are forgetting to forget it, while remembering to reach for the promises of God. Unless the source, reason, and the strategic attacks themselves are identified, overcoming the enemy will become or remain an unending battle.

Be careful not to allow the mind to run free in a brawl of unbridled thinking.

All Chocolate is not Candy

I had an experience as a child, though I can't remember exactly how old I was, that helps to explain the negative and positive aspects of *forgetting, remembering, and reaching.* In any event, one thing is certain: I was too young or too eager to recognize the difference between Ex-Lax and chocolate. Mom was hanging freshly washed clothes on the line in the backyard. I made a mad dash to the kitchen and hurriedly gulped down my delicious treat before she came back into the house.

Without getting into the unpleasant details, what I thought was chocolate candy was not! Let's just say it was more than twenty-five before I was completely delivered from the horrors of that experience. Up until that time, I hated chocolate, but I didn't know why. Each time it touched my tongue, I would quickly spit it out, or worse, but little thought was given to why it was so yucky! I finally connected chocolate with the Ex-Lax ordeal, though the specifics were foggy. It was necessary to remember what happened to forget it and receive deliverance. I eventually added chocolate candies as one of my favorite treats.

Here's the point. I had to remember, or at least understand the experience happened before I could forget it, reach or grow beyond the experience. It is always important to remember what you are forgetting before you can press forward. At that point, *forgetting, remembering, and reaching* empowers you to break free from the past, regardless of how difficult or unkind it may have been.

Experiences can lurk in the background of the mind and influence your daily decisions without you necessarily knowing or recognizing they are there. I'm confident the Ex-Lax experience is not the only memory that may have held me hostage in or to the past, but it is one that caused me to avoid chocolate for more than two decades. The discipline to practice *forgetting, remembering, and reaching* will also help you to recognize whatever it is that is holding you hostage.

Chapter 6

Are You a Loan or a Gift to Your Spouse?

It is natural to cherish precious memories and to revisit some of them during times of sentimental reflections. It is equally desirable to want to become successful and financially secure during one's lifetime. And although each of our value systems differs, everyone cherishes something or the other in a very special way. To be a bit more personal and specific, what is your most cherished or precious possession? Whatever it is, imagine giving it to someone whom you love more than the thing that you are giving. Such a selfless act of love would not create a loss for you, but a gain that each of your lives would be blessed and enriched by. To go a little further, imagine giving or donating a kidney to your spouse, sister, brother, or a total stranger. But instead of fretting over no longer having both kidneys, you are overjoyed that a kidney that was once living in your body is now living in his or hers. The gift would connect the two of you for life, inseparably together.

Jesus shares in Luke 6:38 a spiritual law that applies to every aspect of giving, and if this spiritual law is obeyed, it will meet the needs of both the givers and the receivers. "Give, and [gifts] will be given to you; good measure, pressed down, shaken together, and running over, will they pour into [the pouch formed by] the bosom [of your robe and used as a bag]. For with the measure you deal out [with the measure you use when you confer benefits on others], it will be measured back to you." Insofar as marriage is concerned, a miracle takes place when the husband gives himself to his wife and the wife gives herself to the husband. If each spouse gives himself or herself away to his or her spouse, selfishness is not only replaced by selflessness, but it is eliminated from the marriage altogether. In other words, when spouses surrender personal ownership of themselves to the marriage itself, rights and privileges can no longer separate what God has joined together in holy matrimony.

Remember, a loan, whether short–term or long–term, is conditional with an expiration date. But a gift is permanent and unconditional, with no strings or small print conditions attached. Each spouse, by having surrendered ownership of self, is no longer putting his or her needs first, but rather the spouse's. When your spouse knows you are an unconditional gift and not a conditional loan, love flows freely and continually between the two of you.

If the relationship between spouses is reckoned as a loan, it is conditional at best and at worse, temporary. Anything you receive as a loan does not actually belong to you. Hence the opportunity and freedom to fully enjoy it is limited by time restraints and conditions. Not only that, but you may have to relinquish the loan at a time when you need it the most. So if you are only a loan to your spouse, you are subject to abandon him or her because you, within your own mind, belong to yourself and are likely the apple of your own eye.

Let us not forget to remember that God ordained marriage; the husband and wife are the nucleus of the family, and are commanded by Him to be fruitful and multiply. God's instructions to Adam and Eve to be fruitful and multiply are still His command for the family. However, in today's society, marriage has, in many relationships, taken a backseat to cohabitation or shacking, and having children out-of-wedlock is a much easier task than is rearing and nurturing them. Nonetheless, the responsibility of parents is to provide for their children, and to create a holy atmosphere that teaches them how to learn to hear the voice of God. From within the family nucleus, children are to be taught how to receive and share love in and outside of the family. Children who are taught to love their parents will also learn to love all adults as parents and all children as siblings. Strangers are to be respected as extended family members or neighbors.

Although this book touches on numerous subjects, topics, principles, and scriptures, its focus begins and ends with the family. Everything, whether spoken or inferred, can be traced back to the family. The home environment is the seedbed of love where all the skills, disciplines, and gifts are to be developed in a holy atmosphere within the home.

Love begins at home and spreads abroad.

Get on Board

In a sense of speaking, marriage is a one-way, nonstop, ongoing flight into a foreign country. It is a one-way journey, ordained by God to last as long as husband and wife live. It is nonstop because it must be fed and nourished each day. Therefore, divorce or wanting to desert the marriage in midstream or midflight is not an option to consider. Moreover, it is an ongoing and enduring journey without a get–off or cancelled destination. Again, it is likened to taking a trip into a foreign country where the two of you must necessarily learn a new, encrypted language to communicate and understand each other's needs in the bonds of love, where one plus one equals one, not two.

Also, when visiting a foreign country, you need to learn or at least familiarize yourself with the laws, customs, mores, and traditions of that country. The husband and wife were reared in their particular home environments. Therefore, their upbringing is foreign in comparison to the relationship they are committing to. It is thus crucial that they ask the Holy Spirit to teach them the true meaning of commitment and sacrifice, growth and change, give and take. These are among the necessary steps to help the marriage to grow harmoniously and unconditionally. Most importantly, marriage is a covenanted relationship that requires a much different mindset from that of a single person who is content dating with no intentions of marrying. It requires learning a language of selfless love, free of unhealthy family ties, societal customs, and traditions. Religion and faith play a vital role in the overall growth and development of a marriage.

It is of utmost importance to know that when turbulent trials and tribulations are encountered along the way, the Holy Spirit will instruct you to fasten your seatbelts that are secured when the bonds of love and commitment are tightly joined together. At such a time, He will either take you above or below, through, or around the turbulence spawning on the wings of growth and change, commitment and sacrifice.

When you look out the windows of life through the eyes of God, the eyes of your understanding will be enlightened to see marriage as it was from the beginning. You will also learn to see order amid disorder, and victory where defeat seems certain. With an attitude of gratitude, your enlightened understanding of marriage is transformed and soars on the wings of committed love. With a new or renewed commitment, nothing and no one will be able to separate what God has joined together.

An Encore of Some Foreign Aspects of Marriage

It is fitting to rehash, restate, and add to the metaphor that likens marriage to taking a flight into a foreign country where the environment is unlike anything you have ever experienced. To be more specific, marriage can be likened to two powerful countries merging into a new country different from the old ones. Not only that, but neither country understands the other's language, customs, or traditions. But rather than trying to learn the language of your spouse, commit to creating a new language unique to the two of you.

Various dialects of the new language must include unconditional love, a willingness to listen to heart matters with the heart, and a commitment to never take each other for granted. From within the boundless borders of sacrifice and commitment, talking and listening will lovingly replace arguing and accusing. One of the most foreign aspects of taking flight into this foreign country of marriage is the money management barrier. One prevailing school of thought is that financial issues cause more divorces than unfaithfulness.

Regardless of a country's currency, the lack of money or foolish spending tends to quench the flames of love and affection. In any event, money is money, despite the country's currency. For example, Germany's monetary unit is the Deutsche Mark, Denmark's the krona, Thailand's the baht, South Korea's the won, and the United Kingdom's the pound. So, when traveling to a foreign country, one must learn how to convert his or her currency into that country's. In marriage, the husband and wife must learn how to reconcile their spending habits, as well as their attitudes concerning money, and develop a personal monetary language they both understand. If not, their lack of understanding regarding money in their foreign country of marriage will stunt growth, strangle love, and eventually smother other areas of the marriage.

However, when the Holy Spirit is *piloting* the marriage, He will teach, lead, and protect you until Christ returns and raptures the Church. Therefore, allow Him to navigate you through turbulence encountered during flight into *your* foreign country of holy matrimony. In the meantime, while taking the flight of marriage into its own individual foreign country, devote inflight and lifetime attention to learning and understanding, sharing and speaking the diverse language of love that includes understanding wise money management. Although love conquers all and money is the answer to every need that pertains to money, neither is understood nor mastered without God being at the helm of the husband and wife's lives during every leg of the flight of their marital journey together.

The Past and Present Joined Together at the Proverbial Hip in Time

There is a subtitle in Chapter 7, She Also Has a Story to Tell, about a bag lady who dresses in tattered winter clothing, regardless of the season, and pushes her loaded cart up and down the streets from neighborhood to neighborhood in search of food and throwaways while going nowhere in particular. She will likely never get a chance to tell her story, though she surely has a story to tell.

But unlike the bag lady, Walter and Marie (not their real names) have a story to tell. Although it's Walter who is sharing his point of view about their marriage, his purpose is not to make Marie the villain or himself the victim or hero. He knows Marie also has a story to tell. He believes telling his side of their story will help him shut the door to the past and prayerfully experience a renewed beginning in their marriage. Walter also believes numerous other marriages are dealing with similar situations.

Walter sat down slowly and crossed his legs awkwardly at the ankles, looked to the right toward the floor, pressed his fingers tightly together, took a deep breath, and remained anxious and speechless. The silence filled the room and echoed an eerie silence off the walls for what seemed like several minutes. Still in deep silence, patiently waiting, believing in listening to Walter, whenever he decided to talk, though relating his story to *forgetting, remembering, and reaching* was not going to be an easy task. Even so, it is certain that telling his story will help other couples find their way back to each other. Yet, it will likely be a very difficult task linking *forgetting, remembering, and reaching* together in an inseparably bonding way. The reason is, the memories and experiences Walter needs to forget are part of the reality he is living.

For Walter, forgetting and yet remembering is easier said than done. Nevertheless, he's holding onto the promises of God, reaching out, and praying for strength to endure his marital woes without violating the sanctity of marriage. In short, Walter's marriage uncovers the challenges of *forgetting, remembering, and reaching*, while he struggles not to give up altogether. He has read what the apostle Paul had to say in the following verses. He also knows failure to obey is arguably responsible for some spouses seeking greener grass in forbidden pastures. But let me be very clear – two wrongs do not equal a right, and they are therefore unacceptable excuses for unfaithfulness:

1 Corinthians 7:3-5 The husband should give to his wife her conjugal rights (goodwill, kindness, and what is due her as a wife), and likewise the wife to her husband. **For** the wife does not have [exclusive] authority *and* control over her own body, but the husband [has his rights]; likewise also the husband does not have [exclusive] authority *and* control over his body, but the wife [has her rights]. **Do** not refuse *and* deprive *and* defraud each other [of your due marital rights], except perhaps by mutual consent for a time, so that you may devote yourselves unhindered in prayer. But afterwards resume marital relations, lest Satan tempt you [to sin] through your lack of restraint of sexual desire. [Compare Exod. 19:15.]

The following is a biographical account of Walter's story:

I read or heard someone say that most married couples have sex two or three times per week. One of the reasons I got married was to enjoy sex without feeling dirty or guilty. Perhaps that was a mistake, I don't know! Anyway, sex before our marriage was a blast, and maybe sex before marriage is the reason for the drama about sex after our marriage.

Marie became increasingly indifferent and unwilling to have sex with me. Whenever

I approached her or tried to be romantic, I was spurned, rejected, and accused of being unromantic. Almost every time sex was mentioned, I was accused of having a sex demon. So naturally, I chose not to make mention of sex very often. But even when days, weeks, months, and finally years passed without us being sexually intimate, with the slightest mention of sex, I was still accused of having a sex demon. But I thought to myself, if I had a sex demon, I would have done something by now with that demon!

It's really hard to sleep in the bed with Marie night after night and not be allowed to touch her without causing an argument. At first, I became angry, but that didn't change anything. I thought about thinking about turning to other women, and in all honesty, the thoughts became harder and harder not to think about thinking about. Not only that, but I could tell who was interested in me, though I never tested the waters, but I could tell…

I thought and prayed my way beyond that temptation, yet nothing changed! The entire nightmare was both strange and fascinating in a weird way. Because we seldom had sex, I always hoped that it might take place at any time, so that gave me hope. But at the same time, I dreaded the thought of having sex with Marie because I knew that after that rare time, it would restart the cycle of weeks, days, months, and eventually years passing before the next intimate encounter. So, wanting and not wanting to have sex with Marie was an emotional tug-of-war! Yet nothing changed.

Since I didn't have control over when we might have sex, I learned how not to want to. I'm not saying that was the right thing to do, but it was what I had to do to accept not having sex with her and at the same time resisting thoughts of having sex with someone else. I learned, by not having sex with her, how to appreciate the thought of sexual intimacy in a most godly way. I also learned how not to want to have sex in order not to go astray. At this point, I don't know how to fix things, or if things changed today, I don't know if I know how to get back to the romantic side of things with Marie. I am by no means angry anymore. It's just that I have lost or buried my desire for her. That was necessary for my survival and sanity. I have learned and accepted being a married man living the life of a single person, because the marriage has been derailed by a sexless marital relationship.

But I'm not saying Marie was wrong or that I am right. Or that Marie is right and I am wrong. I am sharing my story with you and praying it will help someone else. I don't believe this is the way marriage should be, but I have accepted Marie's decision. I have learned how not to desire her. I am no longer angry, but this is an ordeal I was not prepared for in marriage. My emotions have spiraled from disbelief to anger to feelings of rejection and unworthiness that worsened from battling temptations to a state of indifference. Nevertheless, I now have the strength to live in these present conditions by forgetting the past and reaching for the future. But of all the possible problems imaginable in marriage, I never thought this would be one. I know God can deliver us, but I

don't know how to unlearn what
I learned that helped me to cope
with the marriage. I'm okay, and
regardless of why it happened, it
happened. To keep from giving
up and walking away, I had to
turn myself off, and now, to be
perfectly honest, I don't know if
I know how to turn myself back
on. I pray God will show me what
to do and empower me to do it.

The thing most challenging about Walter and Marie's marriage, insofar as *forgetting, remembering, and reaching* are concerned, is that they are living in what Walter is trying to forget. Walter is faced with the challenge of forgetting feeling rejected and unloved, and at the same time remembering the instructions of Paul for the husband and wife. Walter believes by faith that he will grow and reach beyond his situation. He is also praying and believing God will bless him and Marie to find their way back to each other.

To restate what Walter is dealing with, he is, on one hand, doing the best he knows how under the circumstances to remain faithful to his wife.

On the other hand, he is enduring the situation by forgetting or looking past Marie's rejection that led to their marriage nose-diving into a cold and *don't touch me* relationship. Walter is struggling with forgetting the past that is part of his present. But he is also remembering his wedding vows, reaching out in hope, and claiming by faith that all things do indeed work together for the good of them that love God, and are called according to His purpose. Nonetheless, Walter's past and present have met at the crossroads of their marital problems that seem likely to become a future reality. Yet he is committed to *forgetting, remembering, and reaching*, despite the unresolved marital stalemate he and Marie are presently living. Walter and Marie's situation is much different from someone forgetting the past that is no longer part of the present.

The only way Walter and Marie can press forward toward *forgetting, remembering, and reaching* is to trust God to deliver them from themselves. But if this were Marie's and not Walter's story, the details would likely be much different. But if they were to tell each other their individual story and commit to renewing their love for each other, God would heal their marriage! I pray God speaks to their hearts, and that they hear and speak heart-to-heart to each other.

In any event, the reason for sharing Walter and Marie's story from Walter's point of view is to help marriages struggling with similar situations. Moreover, it is to stress that *forgetting, remembering, and reaching* are not necessarily easy, but it is doable, and each of us is encouraged to work through the process, regardless of the situation or circumstance. Start with taking baby steps, striding to go from minutes to hours, hours to days, days to months, months to years, and finally, growth and change will become the norm!

If Walter and Marie are willing to embrace the art of forgetting and forgiving, remembering and reaching will catch up with and overtake them. But accepting Christ as your Lord and Savior and getting married are the two most important decisions a person can make in this life. It is therefore understandable that commitment to God and spouse is an unending struggle for the uncommitted to faithfully honor, especially because each is under constant attack from Satan. This need not be the case, though it often is.

And although a sad commentary, far too many couples learn how to be faithful and loving spouses during the twilight years of the marriage. Yet it is seldom discussed openly how captivating and tempting it is when crossing paths with a person from a different generation, and secretly thinking, *"Had I met you when I was your age, we could have had a wonderful life together."* Most of us would like to rethink or unthink at least one thought, undo a decision made, or rekindle a lost love taken for granted. At risk of ignoring the importance of forgetting and reaching, the memory lane many of us are unwilling to go down, because it may dead-end in rekindling forbidden desires. Therefore, the following is the silent voice of many a person shared anonymously by one person, expressed in an editorial narrative that shows how wandering thoughts triggered by unrequited love can affect the heart:

The pilot light on the stove burns, but it quivers in the winds of time that are slowly snuffing it out. The eyes burn, too, though the flame is not as hot and does not burn as long. The stove will heat up, but it is usually left unlit, cold, and unused. The cook now turns the stove on less and less. Perhaps the stove and the cook have grown too unfamiliar with each other in familiar ways. After all, Publilius Syrus said long ago, "Familiarity breeds contempt." *What They Said,* The Ultimate Authoritative Book of Quotations, p. 302.

If the cook only knew how the stove feels and the stove understood the cook's need, they could caringly rekindle their passionate, *culinary* affections for each other. Even so, the stove is, at best, faintly burning with fading and lukewarm longings, while the cook seems content letting the stove rust in the quietness of solitary rejection. But when the stove was a new experience, the cook enjoyed spending time with it, savoring the aromatic delicacies of love's enduring ecstasy. Are the stove and the cook not supposed to be as one? Is not the stove for the cook and the cook for the stove? But now the stove is an object of abject idleness, and the cook seems to have developed a mindset of unattached distancing, having or showing little or no interest in cooking on the stove or eating from the table of love, romance, and commitment.

What happens when the heat no longer fuels the flame? What should the cook do about or with the stove? How should the stove regard its importance or perceived lack of it? The cook has a different point of view, and the stove wants to hear from the cook. Are they not permanent entities of the same household and each other? Perhaps the stove needs to be cared for more lovingly. Maybe the stove needs to develop a renewed sense of blissful appreciation when the cook *turns* it on.

Nonetheless, the stove and the cook continue to remain cold, aloof, and unused.

Chapter 7

Important Keys to *Forgetting, Remembering, and Reaching*

In Genesis 18:10-14, God reveals His plan for Abraham and Sarah to have a child. Understandably, it was natural for Sarah to laugh within herself when she overheard the Lord's promise to bless her and Abraham with a son. Due to their advanced age, their desire for and ability to have sex were mostly gone. Probably their closest encounter with a romantic evening was faint memories of what it was like when the flames of passion were aflame in their hearts. Nonetheless, God promised them a son! And to increase Abraham's faith in the promise, the angel of the Lord asked him a self-examining question of faith-building importance. "Is anything too hard or too wonderful for the Lord?" (Gen. 18:14a). He then reaffirms His promise by assuring Abraham that, "At the appointed time," he would return, quicken Sarah's body, and she would conceive and give birth to the child of promise, Isaac.

We can learn much from God's faithfulness to Abraham and Sarah. But to trust God wholeheartedly, you must be willing to forget what you think you know. Be willing to admit and remember how much bigger God is than your experiences of Him. Do this and reach for the God of impossibilities. When you trust God wholeheartedly, *forgetting, remembering, and reaching* create the manifestation of an unbroken chain of events that empower you to see the unseen. Therefore, commit to living each day of your life in expectancy of receiving the bountiful blessings of God. When you commit to living in the now presence of God, you will not forget to remember that the present is pregnant with the unborn future.

Paul Exemplifies the Power of Forgetting

You may have a past you prefer not to remember, yet it is necessary to remember the past to forget it. However, do not think it strange that you have had experiences that you wish had never happened. You did things that made perfectly good sense at the time, but looking back, you cannot understand what you were thinking when you did what you did.

Regardless, be encouraged! The past is past. You can learn from Saul of Tarsus, whose past, after he became a follower of Christ, haunted him throughout his lifetime. However, Saul's life before and Paul's life after his conversion are equally important in his commitment to press forward. He was victorious over his past because he endured and overcame every trial and tribulation. He understood the importance of *forgetting, remembering, and reaching.*

Unknown in Paul's day, there is a trendy cliché used today by some rational thinking people who'll proudly confess, "I'll forgive, but I won't forget." This is a cliché used by both believers and unbelievers. It seems to suggest you can forgive a person and yet relive, over and over, whatever it was that was done to you. But it is unlikely to have forgiven an offender without having forgotten the offense. So, is it possible to forgive without forgetting the *thing* forgiven? To believe you can forgive and not forget might sound trendy and perhaps slightly religious on the surface. But it is nothing more than a clever trick to hold you and the offender hostage by reminding him or her that he or she is forgiven for something that you will have chosen not to forget. Amazingly, numerous religious sayings have nothing whatsoever to do with God.

Forgiveness means releasing the person without any strings attached, no moral probationary period that requires the person to meet certain conditional dos and don'ts. To forgive is to move beyond the past without using it against the person forgiven. Far too many people are holding themselves hostage in and with their past by holding someone hostage in theirs. To which Booker T. Washington said, "You cannot hold a man down without staying down with him" – The Great Quotations (1971) edited by George Seldes, p. 386. For example, a decision to purposefully stunt a person's growth also stunts yours. The oppressor is also oppressed. Time and energy devoted to hurting someone else also hurt you. That which you take unlawfully from others is lawfully withheld from you. In a sense of speaking, an unforgiving person can be likened to a sentry guarding a prisoner. Whatever the prisoner is locked in, the guard is locked to; both are restrained.

Consider this one also. What if there were a stack of unclaimed money twenty feet from you in the middle of a room? But before you can get to the money, another person leaps on top of you, rendering both of you unable to retrieve the money. Point being, the only way to hinder someone else is to hinder yourself in the process of hindering him or her. This is particularly true when it comes to forgetting, the first step in forgiving. To forgive is to forget to remember what you are forgetting and forgiving. Remembering and forgetting are a necessary step in reaching and receiving.

Paul speaks of forgetting the past and reaching for the short-lived present that is always giving way to the future. It is not known if Paul forgot everything that he was forgetting, but he certainly lived a life of forgetting and reaching. In the course of forgetting, he was remembering to let go of the past, and reaching for the promises of God in the present, a stepping-stone into the future. For Paul to embrace and fulfill the high or upward calling of God in Christ Jesus, he accepted the fact that Christ had forgiven him. He also understood the importance of forgiving himself for his former life, which he dedicated to persecuting the church. He had to forgive others as well, even if they were unwilling to forgive him. The fact that Paul was a praying man empowered him to press forward. He, by forgetting and reaching, understood how to overcome his trials and tribulations.

It is, in fact, impossible to be forgiven if you are unwilling to forgive. Jesus shares this truth with clarity in Matthew 6:14-15, "For if you forgive people their trespasses [their reckless and willful sins, leaving them, letting them go, and giving up resentment], your heavenly Father will also forgive you. But if you do not forgive others their trespasses [their reckless and willful sins, leaving them, letting them go, and giving up resentment], neither will your Father forgive you your trespasses." Forgiveness is an act of giving, and Luke 6:38 teaches that giving has a built-in principle that touches every area of life. "Give, and [gifts] will be given to you; good measure, pressed down, shaken together, and running over, will they pour into [the pouch formed by] the bosom [of your robe used as a bag]. For with the measure you deal out [with the measure you use when you confer benefits on others], it will be measured back to you." In other words, if you refuse to forgive others of their trespasses, God will not forgive you of your trespasses. If you forgive sparingly, you will be forgiven sparingly. Also, whatever is given sparingly will be received sparingly. God will use the same measuring stick of right and wrong on you that you use on others.

The Unforgiving is Un-forgiven

Love and forgiveness are inseparable attributes of God and characteristic of the children of God. The importance of forgiving is taught and made clear throughout the Bible. The following is one of many parables Jesus used to teach on forgiveness, as well as the consequences of not forgiving. Peter asked Jesus a question concerning forgiveness, a question that the other disciples were probably unwilling to ask, though they likely wanted to know. It's a blessing to have someone in the classroom, in the family, on the job, in the political arena, or in the church, willing to ask the questions that everyone else is unwilling to ask.

In any event, whatever Peter wanted to know, he asked. "Then Peter came up to Him and said, Lord, how many times may my brother sin against me and I forgive him and let it go? [As many as] up to seven times?" (Matt. 18:21.) Peter was certain that forgiving someone seven times was a loving and righteous thing to do, a high and mighty act of holiness. However, in verse 22, "Jesus answered him, I tell you, not up to seven times, but seventy times seven!" [Compare Gen. 4:24.] Seventy times seven equals 490, or an indefinite number of times. Therefore, the number of times you are commanded to forgive is without number. Furthermore, keeping a record of your good deeds amounts to erecting a stumbling block between you and God. Also, 490 is an important number in "The Seventy-Week Prophecy" given to the prophet in Daniel 9:24. In his prophecy, each week represents seven years, and seven times seventy equals 490. I believe the 490 in Matthew 18:22 and Daniel 9:24 is somehow interrelated.

Jesus's answer probably shocked Peter to the core of his religious bones. Nonetheless, Jesus continued to teach on the diverse depths of forgiveness. In verses 23–24, He explains the king's response to his servant's debt. "Therefore the kingdom of heaven is like a human king who wished to settle accounts with his attendants. When he began the accounting, one was brought to him who owed him 10,000 talents [probably about $10,000,000."]

The scripture does not say whether the talents were silver or gold, though they were likely gold. Regardless, it was a debt that was impossible for him to repay, but verses 25–27 illustrate the boundless depth of forgiveness: "And because he could not pay, his master ordered him to be sold, with his wife and his children and everything that he possessed, and payment to be made. So the attendant fell on his knees, begging him, Have patience with me and **I** will pay you everything. And the master's heart was moved with compassion, and he released him and forgave him [cancelling] the debt."

It is ungodly to want someone to do for you the very thing you are unwilling to do for someone else. For example, people who do not want to be talked about, lied on, or to, will spread vicious rumors and lies without giving it a second thought. Life is, in many ways, like a spiritual boomerang: What you do returns to you, be it blessings or curses. In other words, what goes around comes around, or to be more biblically correct, we are told in Galatians 6:7 "Do not be deceived *and* deluded *and* misled; God will not allow Himself to be sneered at (scorned, disdained, or mocked by mere pretensions or professions, or by His percepts being set aside). [He inevitably deludes himself who attempts to delude God.] For whatever a man sows, that *and* that only is what he will reap."

The servant appealed to the king for mercy, and the king was very merciful and forgave the huge debt. Sadly, it is quite easy to forget to remember how gracious and merciful God is to us each day. In verse 28 of Matthew, the attendant or servant who was forgiven a huge debt was unwilling to forgive a fellow attendant of a much smaller debt. "But the same attendant, as he went out, found one of his fellow attendants who owed him a hundred denarii [about twenty dollars]; and he caught him by the throat and said, Pay what you owe!"

- The first servant had a debt beyond his ability or means to repay.
- The second servant owed the first servant very little.
- The first servant was forgiven a huge debt, but was unwilling to forgive a fellow servant of a much smaller debt.
- God has forgiven the believer a debt too great to repay, even if he or she possessed the entire wealth of the world.
- God has forgiven you and me a debt we could not pay or settle.
- It is therefore a must that we forgive others their debts or trespasses committed against us, that are small and petty in comparison to the debt God has forgiven us, paid for and cancelled by Jesus on the cross.
- If we refuse to forgive, regardless of the reason or justification, it is still inexcusable and unacceptable in the eyes of God.

He Who Expects Kindness
Must Show Kindness

Listen to the words of Jesus recorded in Matthew 7:12: "So then, whatever you desire that others would do to and for you, even so do also to and for them, for this is (sums up) the Law and the Prophets." Is it not strange that murderers who kill and commit wicked acts of violence will do all they can to avoid prison or the death penalty? Killers, who desire to live, though they have killed others, are undeniable proof that they value the precious gift of life. If everyone valued the sanctity of life, suicide, violence, and the high rate of murder would decrease overnight.

Most disagreements could be settled or avoided altogether if love, mercy, and grace were the peacemakers. Thus, *forgetting, remembering, and reaching* are important components to burying the past, breathing new life into the present, and embracing the manifold blessings of God for the future. So rejoice and obey the divine commands of God, fulfill your calling, and experience His glorious presence.

We cannot excuse ourselves for doing wrong by claiming we didn't know.

Although some mistakes and sinful acts may have been committed out of ignorance, we should learn not to try to justify other mistakes and sins by claiming we didn't know. Each of us has made mistakes that we should learn from and not repeat. In other words, when you learn better, do better, or suffer the consequences of not *forgetting, remembering, and reaching*. Jesus makes this truth clear in Luke 12:48, "But he who did not know and did things worthy of a beating shall be beaten with few [lashes]. For everyone to whom much is given, of him shall much be required; and of him to whom men entrust much, they will require *and* demand all the more."

Please do not forget to remember that the day of reckoning is coming. Each of us will one day, real soon, be blessed or punished for our actions or inactions, be they right or wrong. A day of reckoning and accountability is coming.

The Eternal Blessings of *Forgetting, Remembering, and Reaching*

Spiritual growth and empowerment are attained when *forgetting, remembering, and reaching* are a learned discipline, so make it a practice to use it daily. Moreover, they are also closely related, important in every chapter of life. They not only teach principles of giving and receiving, but also how to overcome trials and tribulations by *forgetting, remembering, and reaching*.

What if, for example, you were critically ill, and the doctors told you there is no cure for your condition? To have the faith to believe you would not die in a few days, you would need to forget to remember to accept the diagnosis as the final word, while remembering not to forget the promises of God. You would need to see beyond what it looks like, reach into the faith realm, and confess the Word of God for healing and deliverance. If this example were a real situation, you would need to remember there is a vast difference between receiving healing and walking in your healing or deliverance.

However, refusing to forget, whether it is nursing sicknesses, hurts, or disappointments, will likely discourage you from reaching or pressing forward. So forgetting to remember involves a decision not to revive the past. If not, it clouds the present, blinds your spiritual eyes, and allows the past to resurface and affect your future. When this happens, your spiritual eyes are blinded to the promises of God received in the present for the future. Allow Paul's commitment in Philippians 3:13b to become your commitment:

"Forgetting what lies behind and straining forward to what lies ahead."

But what exactly is it you need to forget? Everything and anything that is holding you down, trying and vying to pull you back into the past! Learn to forget your victories and defeats. Divorce yourself from the past. Do not allow it to hold you hostage in the present and prevent you from pressing forward and embracing future promises of God. It is possible, as is often the case, to go through the motions of doing or not doing, without actually doing what needs to be done. Also, resist the temptation of going nowhere fast! Busyness does not necessarily mean effective and meaningful progress.

Marking Time is a Waste of Time

Everything has a purpose. It is meaningless to do something just for the sake of doing it. When I was in the US Army, we were routinely ordered to jog or march. At other times, we were instructed to mark time. The dictionary's definition of mark time – "To keep the time of a marching step by moving the feet alternately without advancing or to maintain a static state of readiness." When marking time, the body is busy with physical motions without any forward progress. Nevertheless, energy, effort, and time are used to keep the body in a state of constant motion, whether moving or mimicking movement from a stationary position.

Refusing to forget, remember, and to reach or press forward can be likened, in many ways, to marking time. Point being, it is difficult to be reaching without forgetting and remembering, though you may go through the motions of doing so. To forget is to unload dead baggage; to remember is to seek and receive the promises of God. To reach is to stop marking time, remembering past hurts and disappointments that you cannot unlive, or victories you cannot relive. Living in the now will get your Egypt experiences of the past out of you and you out of your Egypt memories into the land of the promises, flowing with milk and honey.

On the other hand, do not fool yourself into believing you can set on the sidelines of life, and wait for things to somehow work themselves out. If you choose to do *nothing*, an unwanted *something* will come out of your not doing. A do-nothing decision equals not *forgetting, remembering, and reaching*. It is to surrender into the arms of the enemy without realizing how dangerous it is to believe things will somehow work themselves out. The notion that not taking any action prevents unwanted events from taking place is untrue. Doing *nothing* about *something* causes *nothing* to become a worthless *something*. The sower of idleness will reap more of the nothing sown. It is a lot like marking time or marching in place, using energy doing nothing that could have been used doing something. Inert motion without purposeful action equals a sum total of nothing!

Imitate Paul's Model of Forgetting

You breathed yesterday. Pray you will be breathing tomorrow. Thank God you are breathing right now, today! What you did or plan to do is not nearly as important as what you are doing. The labor that yields fruit comes from the work you did today. To make sure you are living life in the now, commit to practicing *forgetting, remembering, and reaching.* Today is always right now.

Paul lived life forgetting. It was as much a part of his life as breathing! Philippians 3:13 is a reminder of the importance of committing to practicing forgetting and reaching. "I do not consider, brethren, that I have captured *and* made it my own [yet]; but one thing **I** do [it is my one aspiration]: forgetting what lies behind and straining forward to what lies ahead."

Paul regarded forgetting and reaching as a single process. In other words, it is impossible to be reaching without forgetting because forgetting is the proof you are reaching. Paul knew forgetting his former life, forgiven by Christ, was the only way he could press forward toward the mark for the prize of the high or upward calling of God in Christ Jesus. Although often challenged to justify or defend his life in Christ, Paul did not allow his past to hold him hostage. His accusers, abusers, and doubters, however, wanted him to remember the things that he was committed to forgetting, although he had not fully apprehended the grace and mercy for which he had not yet fully attained. Remembering the risen Christ and the upward calling of God was reason enough for Paul to continue forgetting and reaching. Although he persecuted the church and acted out of ignorance, and he never tried to use that to excuse or justify himself. He did not allow what he did in the past stop him from preaching Christ, and Him crucified.

We can learn from Paul to play the metaphoric hand we are dealt, retained, or that we dealt to ourselves, proverbially speaking. Either way, life is lived without breaks, timeouts, or intermissions. Life does not take days off, vacations, holidays, or sick leaves. Ready or not, life is now! But had Paul's life and ministry not been included in the Bible, we would not have been blessed to learn life-changing lessons from this mighty man of God.

Rewind, Pause, Fast–Forward

When a movie is being shot, the set and location are carefully selected to capture or portray its intended theme or message. Stunt persons and look-alikes are sometimes used as doubles for the superstars. Props and riveting scenes are created to captivate the audience. Yes. The cinema can create unrealistic ideas and lifestyles, particularly harmful to the vulnerable minds of the young and innocent. During filming, scenes are shot and reshot, and the finished product is edited before it is released to an audience to make sure it portrays the intended message.

Once the film is a finished product and available for viewing in home, it can be watched with the touch of a button or the flip of a switch. With modern technology, you have numerous options at your disposal. For example, you can opt to watch certain scenes and skip others. You can rewind and watch certain scenes over and over, or you can fast-forward and not watch others.

But on another note, it is arguably possible for actors to play so many different characters until they lose touch with themselves and reality. It might be much easer to play a character role, and become someone else rather than being true to one's self. To which William Shakespeare said, "All the world's a stage, and all the men and women merely players" – *POCKET BOOKS,* a division of Simon & Schuster, Inc., p. 377. Although Shakespeare's observation is not biblical, he admittedly had a point.

However, looking at Shakespeare's comment from a biblical perspective identifies several meaningful parallels between the world and a stage. One meaning for the *world* has to do with the secular system and the people who are part of it. And of course *stage* is a raised platform for thespians or actors to perform on, though acting is not limited to the stage. It extends, to varying degrees, into the lives of people from all walks of life. Some people live to act as a career. Others act or perform and live by a set of self-styled survival rules of conduct that are outside the norm, especially when not leaning and depending on God. Whether the performances take place on stage, in the cinema, or on the streets of hard knocks, thespians or actors often take on the persona of the person or situation they are portraying, instead of being the person God created them to be. Although acting is indeed a career choice for some, for others it is a craving obsession, developed from a troublesome sense of despair of unwelcome feelings infused with unsettled frustrations that are crying out to be heard, though the chosen paths often take them further away from the callings of the heart.

Admittedly, comparing, rather than discussing the world as that of a stage, is a far shift from *forgetting, remembering, and reaching*. Yet, the way life is lived by some people has a lot to do with whether or not *forgetting, remembering, and reaching* are practiced. But regarding character acting, it allows performers, not limited to professional actors, to play or pretend to be someone else while showcasing and disguising himself or herself artistically. It's a way of hiding in plain sight, exposing one's true self without being unmasked. It is a type of concealed nakedness uncovered and expressed openly that is hidden on the silver screen. It's a perfect cover to pretend to be someone other than who you are without exposing your identity to everyone to see. Acting provides a platform for *actors,* on and off stage, to portray a person that they might want to be, but are unwilling to be, for fear of being exposed as that person.

The truth of the matter, life is much larger than the small stage it is lived by people in this world who are estranged from the love of God. Nonetheless, acting allows the lives of artists to remain hidden on the silver screen in the shadows of dramatic performances. Nevertheless, each of us is searching, whether knowingly or unknowingly, purposefully or randomly, for our true selves while facing the uncertain dangers of losing our way on the world's stage in search of our identity and purpose in life.

Before continuing, please allow me to insert a disclaimer. Neither actors nor acting is being criticized. The cinema has brought many tragedies and injustices to light that may have otherwise remained hidden. The truth to grasp from this discussion is that not only acting, but with most professions, there is an innate danger of being steered away from your true calling in God. It's just that the stage makes or creates an alluring opportunity to do so.

Precious Diamonds in the Rough

In Psalm 139:14 (KJV) it is written, "I will praise thee; for I am fearfully *and* wonderfully made:

marvelous *are* thy works; and *that* my soul knoweth right well." The essence of this truth pulsates in the heart of every human being. Even if you reject or do not know your true identity, the heart knows what the mind might reject or not know. We are created to be more than conquerors, but we must commit to being the conqueror or by default, the conquered. Please don't sacrifice eternity with God for five minutes of fame and fortune in this world. To which Jesus gives a stern warning in Mark 8:36, "For what does it profit a man to gain the whole world, and forfeit his life [in the eternal kingdom of God]?"

When Jesus talked to the Pharisees, He sometimes referred to them as hypocrites and pretenders. This observation is not meant to attack whether art imitates life or life imitates art, and neither is it to pass judgment on actors and performers. But far too many people are living their lives as if they are on stage. Arguably, anyone who is not *forgetting, remembering, and reaching* is hindering his or her spiritual growth.

Nonetheless, there are chapters of unforgettable memories and experiences in most of our lives that we would like to rewind, pause, fast-forward, or rewrite altogether. Wow! Wouldn't life be simply wonderful if it could be rewound and the lives of loved ones extended or paused, to delay sickness or death? What if life could be fast–forwarded past the reality of death to the Rapture? Despite these what ifs, life is not an electronic devise that can be controlled with the flip of a switch. If it were, though it can never be, some of us would find *something* to complain about. However, neither time nor life can be rewound, paused, or fast–forwarded. Therefore, commit your whole life to Christ and live without second-guessing what the past could have been, or complaining about what the present is not, or fearing what the future might be. Live today, today!

Paul shares his distinguished life, before and after meeting Christ on the Damascus road, to teach us the importance of living today, today. He was circumcised on the eighth day of the stock of Israel, of the prestigious tribe of Benjamin, a bona fide Hebrew of the Hebrews, a Pharisee who obeyed the Law and persecuted the church, but who was blameless according to the Law. Moreover, he sat at the feet of Gamaliel, who was a leading Jewish rabbi. Yes! Paul was highly privileged and successful. His life was seemingly perfect, the envy of his peers, but everything changed when he met Christ on the Damascus road. Although Paul often shared his testimony, he never looked or desired to go back. He learned from his past and used that knowledge and wisdom to teach the beloved saints the transforming power of God in Christ Jesus.

This One Thing I Do, Forgetting and Reaching

The demands of life, working, rearing children, schoolwork, housework, yard work, and caring for the elderly, to name a few, require the ability to balance these responsibilities with everything else. However, it is believed by some that multitasking is unhealthy and perhaps even unproductive, though some of us are very effective at performing several tasks at a time. But regardless of the number of tasks you can perform or master at once, it is best and more useful, from a spiritual perspective, to develop a single–minded approach to perfecting or living a life pleasing to God. Despite the number of tasks a person can perform at a time varies, it is better to skillfully and effectively perform one task at a time, rather than trying to perform several jobs at the same time.

Not only did Paul focus on the single commitment of forgetting and reaching, his sense of urgency stresses the utmost importance of single-mindedness. Paul understood a confused or conflicted mind is an ineffective mind. That is, the mind is, in many ways, similar to that of a recording device with a rewind and replay feature. How often do you *rewind,* go down memory lane, and replay an experience, over and over? The problem with rewinding and replaying memories is that life is lived in real time. So, whenever you rewind and replay past joys or sorrows in a longing or regretful way, you are preventing yourself from experiencing life in the present.

You can perhaps temporarily escape the reality of life by pausing mentally and reflecting on the past. It's okay to pause and to reflect, if it helps you to fine–tune your priorities with a sense of direction and urgency. Wisdom and knowledge gleaned from the past can help to prepare you for the future and prevent you from replaying and repeating past mistakes. But if the past is left unresolved, you will likely repeat it sooner or later.

Be careful not to rewind and replay old memories and experiences in an attempt to replace the present with them. Unlike the shooting of a movie or some type of recording, the past cannot be edited or rewritten after it has passed. As life unfolds, it moves on to the next frame of events. It is therefore important to say what you mean and to do what it is you need to do. Believe it or not, but you cannot undo or unsay what you did or said, though you can make amends or atonements for things said or done.

To reiterate, recorded movies can be rewound and replayed, but this is not an option available to us with life. You can think beforehand about what you will say or do. You can even practice and rehearse what you will say or do, but you cannot edit, rehearse, or relive the past after the fact. Any attempt to pause life is dangerous and akin to trying to avoid living life. Decisions made in the past affect decisions that must be made in the present. Although you cannot change past decisions and all of their consequences, you can learn important lessons by forgetting and releasing them into the arms of grace and mercy. Forgetting is an act of forgiving similar to using the delete button on an electronic device. When you delete a previously recorded movie, message, or cellphone number, your action suggest you no longer have need of it, though it remains in existence someplace else. It does means, however, that you have finished or ended your real or imagined bond with it or that person. In any case, letting go of past memories and experiences does not mean they cease to exist as lessons learned. It means they no longer occupy your mind or heart in a confining way. They have been dethroned and the promises and purposes of God enthroned.

Wanting to rewind, replay, pause, or fast-forward life is a waste of time. Forgetting frees you to live your life now in the presence of God. You can rethink what you have experienced, but you cannot live in the present and relive the past at the same time. Moreover, trying to delete or forget previous experiences do not cancel the fact that they took place, but you can put the past to rest. The power and influence of the past are to be built upon, but avoid trying to relive it. The crux of forgetting and remembering frees you to reach for the promises of God. Forgetting is also an act of forgiving, a choice to love unconditionally. The unmerited favor of God's grace and mercy empowers you to be gracious and merciful to others.

Still, life cannot be rewound. It does not have a rewind button. If life had a rewind button, some things done in the past would obviously not have been done or repeated, and other things would have been done better and more lovingly. Some unlearned lessons would have been learned, and other experiences would have been avoided altogether had the right decisions been made in the first place. But at the same time, had we not experienced the things that we have, we probably would not have learned the lessons learned. Regardless of your present situation, Jesus is the resurrection and the life. Allow Him to make all things new in you from a spiritual perspective.

On the other hand, would you be you, had you not become the person you are? You can't honestly say, because you are who you are. But God knows. You cannot now travel the path that was not taken, so where do you go from here? Even if you took the wrong road or the road less traveled, God is leading you to where He desires you to be. This is true despite how hopeless you may feel, regardless of how far you may have veered off the path of righteousness and purpose.

For example, the sun, because of its location in the Heavens, shines upon all the earth, even when clouds hide it from view. The Son, seated at the right hand of God in glory, shines His grace and mercy down from the Heavens on you and me, even though we may refuse to bask in it, because we are unable to see the hand of God working on our behalf. Yes! You may have lost your way; nevertheless, always remember the eyes of the Lord run patiently throughout the whole earth to show Himself strong to everyone that is *forgetting, remembering, and reaching* for the upward or high calling of God in Christ Jesus.

But it's okay to mentally rewind and recall the past as a building block. Pause, and reflect on previous experiences as a mental marker, or fast–forward in preparedness to embrace divine opportunities for the future. But do not allow the thought of rewinding, replaying, pausing, or fast–forwarding to replace living life in real time. Finally, the term, real time, is used repeatedly to remind us that whatever we do or do not, is done in the present.

What's Your Story?

Everyone has a story to tell, but most of us do not get the chance to tell ours. The rich, famous, and successful are privileged with opportunities to tell their stories, and are highly admired by the not-so-rich, famous, or successful. One of many reasons for admiring the privileged is that it's a way of idolizing our untapped potential in them. It is also widely believed that success and moral goodness are the same, though this is not necessarily true across the board.

Arguably, the main difference between the well-known and the lesser-known is that the well–known are in a better position to tell their story. It is also fairly easy for some of us to live our unfulfilled dreams and aspirations through them. Nonetheless, everyone has a story to tell. The drug addict, the prostitute, the child molester, they too have a story to tell. I am by no means suggesting people who do horrible things to others and themselves are to be admired and not punished for what they did. I am simply saying, everyone has a story to tell, and important lessons can be learned from people, be they role models or not. You can learn from others what to do, as well as what not to do.

Take Legions, for example, the Bible does not tell us why he was full of demons or how he lived after he was delivered. The Bible does tell us that when Jesus delivered him, he was immediately made a new person who wanted to follow Jesus. But Jesus told him to go home to his family and friends and show them how merciful Jesus had been to him. Jesus delivered Legions, the demoniac man, and everyone He delivers has a story to tell.

Everyone has a Story to Tell

Most of us are usually the hero or the victim in our story. Both successful and unsuccessful people have at least one thing in common: time and effort were devoted to becoming who they are. The lives of the successful are often the subject of movies, films, documentaries, bestselling books, and advertising campaigns. The masses are understandably captivated by people in the spotlight, and are often drawn into their world where they live their unfulfilled dreams and desires through them. However, wealth and fame does not guarantee happiness, and neither are the rich and powerful necessarily pillars of the community who can be trusted and admired as role models. It has been said that anyone who believes money is the source of happiness probably has never had it.

Nonetheless, the average person, whoever he or she is, will purchase pricey tickets to see, hear, or meet persons who are living life in the spotlight. You can learn from successful people how to become successful, or at least how to go about seeking success. Believe it or not, but the person on Skid Row can probably tell you how not to end up on Skid Row. Each of us has a story to tell that can help others, but we may not get the chance to tell it. Whether successful or unsuccessful, rich or poor, living in a mansion or on skid row, each of us has invested time and effort in the creation and development of our story. Whether precious time is used doing something important or nothing of importance, it contributes to developing good or bad habits with reciprocal outcomes. Each person, one way or the other, invests time in something that may or may not have been devoted to *forgetting, remembering, and reaching* as a catalyst for change. For example, energy is used to shadowbox, that is, box with an imaginary opponent, or to spar in the ring with a bona fide fighter. The difference between shadowboxing and sparring is that an imaginary opponent can't hit you, but a real opponent can and will!

The Smartest or the Gifted Are Not Always the Most Successful

Intelligence, success, and happiness do not necessarily go hand in hand. Some people have failed miserably in life, while many with less natural abilities have become very successful. On another note, it is likely true that almost everyone has a touch of untapped, undiscovered, or undeveloped ability, but discovering and using it is an entirely different matter.

Speaking of untapped ability, three brothers were gifted basketball players who lived in a duplex in a low–income neighborhood. A tall wire fence separated their backyard from the basketball court on the school campus. The location of their home to the school was ideal. It gave them opportunities to play basketball practically anytime they wanted to. The brothers were par excellence basketball players with extraordinary skills difficult to describe. Whether watching them play, playing with or against them, their display of skills was simply amazing. Their dribbling routines looked as if they had been created and choreographed by a movie producer, edited to perfection. The ball and their hands seemed to have been the same. They moved on the court like ballerinas or acrobatic performers that causing the persons defending them to become woozy in the head and wobbly on their feet. Not only that, but the brothers would skillfully glide through midair, defying the law of gravity, and putting spins or English on the ball that only elite NBA players can do. Had they become NBA players, they would have changed the game before the game was changed.

But they did not become NBA players, and there are probably lots of reasons why they didn't. It may have been a lack of ambition, or perhaps they were never in the right place at the right time. Yet what they could do with a basketball was simply magical. They did not usually play on the same team together, but it was always entertaining watching them play the game. Not only were they highly skilled with their unusual abilities, but they also confused and embarrassed the defense while making lots of noise at the same time.

Action Speaks Louder than Words

In this book, you are constantly being reminded of the importance of *forgetting, remembering, and reaching.* Yet I am remembering and sharing experiences that you may think should have been forgotten. After all, they cannot be relived, so why talk about dreams and goals that are part of the past that cannot be revived and relived in the present, and should therefore be forgotten? Right? Right!

But they are forgotten, insofar as wanting or desiring to relive them in the present. What was done or not done in the past is no longer an active part of the present. The purpose of remembering is to share acquired wisdom and learned knowledge gleaned from them. It is a matter of reaching for the blessings available in the present by utilizing endowed wisdom and learned knowledge from the past.

It is also a matter of separating what is from what was. Remembering the time and effort devoted to past goals and dreams helps learn how to devote quality time and effort to reaching for what is achievable in the present. Most important of all, recognizing God is the center of our life cannot be overemphasized. There are, however, generations of people from all walks of life who are unknowingly longing for God.

Sadly, they are numbing their longings with sex, drugs, and grappling for power. The pursuit of wealth and fame is often sought through acts of violence, hatred, and self-destructive behavior that are harmful to both the victimizer and the victim.

When, and if, these elusive dreams, goals, and passions are obtained, the seekers learn, often to their surprise, that fame, success, and wealth neither fill nor satisfy their longings. It is often learned after the fact that the chase did not fulfill the needs or desires. In other words, the chase may turn out to be likened to that of a dog chasing a car. The driver knows the dog can't drive, but that doesn't stop the dog from chasing the car.

Wealth and Poverty Mean Different Things to Different People

The reason for discussing successful and unsuccessful people, the well–known and the mostly unknown, the shakers and the shapers, the winners and the losers, is not to praise or to criticize them. It's only a reminder that everyone has a story to tell that's not always told. Be sure to seize every opportunity to listen to both the well–known and the lesser-known because important lessons can be learned from both.

Whether in the spotlight or the shadows, everyone has a story to tell.

She Also Has a Story to Tell

It's late October, high noon, and the temperature is around 86 degrees. The bag lady, seen daily roaming the neighborhoods from street to street, was dressed in her usual winter gear. Her shopping buggy is overloaded, rattling, and shaking from badly worn wheels. Several garbage bags full of stuff are probably the total of her life's possessions. Was she headed to a particular place or no place in particular? What decisions or circumstances led her to where she was and who she is? Where does she sleep? Does she sleep at all? Who is the real person buried deeply within this person who is always going to and fro? Does she talk, and if she does, with whom and about what?

Although worn and torn by the years, she was once someone's beautiful child who was born with dreams and aspirations. What role, if any, did *forgetting, remembering, and reaching* play in her life? Was it her childhood dream to become a bag lady? Of course not! Only God knows what happened along her highway of life, but sometimes a single decision can set in motion a series of life-changing events.

Here's the point. Stop and think about your most pressing need or situation. Now think about the person begging for money or handouts on the corner. What about the person who does not eat meals from a kitchen table or a fancy restaurant, but from the nearest Dumpster? Or, the homeless people who will make their bed beneath a bridge or in an abandoned building tonight. None of these people planned the life they are living. Although con artists will sometimes station themselves on the corners and prey on passersby, others on those same corners are in desperate need. If you're led to help and the person is a con artist, God will bless you and deal with him or her because everyone's deeds will reproduce after their kind. However, you may think the beggar on the corner will use the money to buy alcohol, and that's sometimes true. But if you were homeless and had to sleep under a bridge tonight, you too would want *something* to help deal with the weather.

To varying degrees, the seemingly hopeless conditions of some people are the result of not practicing *forgetting, remembering, and reaching*; a discipline each of us is encouraged to learn and to practice along life's journey.

I Promised Myself not to be Like Dad

My childhood was interesting from a religious point of view. I was a member of a Baptist church. My mother, who was a lifelong member of The Church of God in Christ, often took my younger brother and me to church with her to perhaps babysit us. At other times, my aunt, who was a Methodist, took me to church with her. I have fond memories of each church experience. Being exposed to these three different denominations taught me not to develop religious biases.

Mom accepted Christ and was filled with the Holy Ghost at the age of thirteen. On the other hand, Dad was, based on his lifestyle, a sinner who did not attend church. The only time he was ever in a church, to my knowledge, was when the pallbearers carried him in for his funeral. In all honesty, I now often wonder why they married. It is somewhat of a mystery to me, but looking at things from a broader perspective, it is difficult to figure out why certain people marry each other.

My Dad was an interesting person for many reasons. Mom loved each of her children the same. Dad, for some unknown reason, favored me. He was an uneducated intellect who enjoyed reading the newspaper and drawing sketches of horses. Mom, less educated than he, enjoyed drawing beautiful flowers from memory.

But back to Papa, who was also a womanizer and a career alcoholic. He was oftentimes too drunk to get into the house without help, unable to undress, or go to the bathroom, and often ended up wetting himself. In any event, alcohol destroyed his ability and desire to work. He would quit or get fired, leaving him unable to help support the family. However, not working did not stop him from drinking. Whenever he lacked money to buy corn whiskey from Doll, the neighborhood bootlegger, who lived less than a five-minute walk from our home, he stole whatever he could sneak out of the house with. Some of the things traded were eventually returned. I can't remember if we had to pay Doll for them, or if she returned them out of the *goodness* of her heart. He would, from time to time, stop drinking for a little while, but his drinking led to psoriasis of the liver and death at age 63.

When I think back on things, Dad was unhappy and trapped in a world of drunkenness that he created. Oftentimes, he was irritable and unkind to Mom, but he was never physically abusive for fear of our stepping in. Whenever Mom grew tired of his ranting and raving, she sang gospel songs, spoke in tongues, and praised God. Her praise and worship always caused him to take flight. He was a sinner, and Mom a saint. In all honesty, Mom and Dad seemed perfectly imperfect for each other. Only God knows why they married. He was a smooth talker, so he may have charmed her off her feet.

At the age of ten, Dad gave me a sip of his Falstaff beer. I didn't ask for it, and I don't know why he gave it to me. All I know is that it was nasty, my first and last sip until I was twenty-one and in the US Army. To fast-forward, after four months of training, I was shipped to Germany, where beer was part of the culture. After three years, I was discharged, returned home, and graduated from drinking beer to stronger stuff.

Nonetheless, I was determined not to become a drunk like Dad. I was usually the designated driver when we went partying. It was believed at the time that I was a responsible drinker and driver, partly because I developed a way to gauge my level of drunkenness. As soon as we entered a club, I would find a picture or something on a faraway wall, study its clarity, and my ability to see the words. Whenever whatever was no longer clear and easy to read, that was my cue that the alcohol was dulling my senses and perception. At that point, I either stopped drinking altogether or drank less and slower. Sometimes, I crossed my threshold of responsible drinking, yet I was determined not to be like Dad. With youth, determination, and the hand of God, unknown to me at the time, was upon me. I was always able to drive and do the things that a sober person could do. Although I was a hot-rodder, I didn't usually mix hot-rodding and drinking. Many times I was probably legally drunk, but I was never ticketed or had an accident. I thank God for looking out for me when I wasn't looking out for myself. Breathalyzers had not been invented, or at least they weren't being used by law enforcement in our city. So whenever stopped and questioned by the police, I was able to dodge the bullet, so to speak.

With the passing of the years, it became obvious that if I continued doing what I was doing, I was headed to where my Dad's life dead–ended. If I continued drinking, I was going to do the very thing I promised myself I would not: become an alcoholic like Dad! So, with some willpower, but mostly when God showed me the folly of believing I would not become the person that I was working on becoming, my drinking went from less to none. But I'm not sharing this to speak negatively about my deceased father, but rather to remind you that the only way to overcome a habit is to stop feeding the habit.

Most importantly, valuable lessons can be learned from every experience. I learned from my Dad not to do or to become what he became, an alcoholic. Here's a surefire way to overcome whatever it is you need or desire to overcome. If you are a liar or a drunk, for example, don't promise God or yourself that you will never tell another lie or take another drink. Make a promise to yourself that you will not drink or lie today, and ask God to help you to keep that promise. Make promises from day to day. Whatever you do or do not do, it will be done or not done today. Learn to make big strides in small steps. In the process of growing, learn to forget your failures, remember the goal, and commit to reaching it. Again, make big strides in small steps.

Negatives and Positives

More often than not, the words *negative* and *positive* are used in *bad* and *good* ways. When applying for a job, you hope and pray the interviewer will rate you to be a positive, not a negative applicant. Most of us prefer relationships with positive, not negative people. You also likely prefer to maintain a positive outlook on life in general instead of a negative or doomsday attitude. But you certainly don't want to have a negative balance in your checking or savings account. If we do not listen carefully and think thoughtfully before speaking, the mere mention of the word *negative* may not make a *positive* impression.

But on the other hand, when given a battery of medical tests, you pray they are all negative. In this case, negative is good and positive is bad. However, now that we are learning how to live and survive a COVID-19 pandemic, if tested for the virus, you certainly want to receive a negative, not a positive reading. So the importance of receiving a negative or positive report varies, depending on the situation or circumstance.

But insofar as my Dad's drinking was concerned, it was a negative that produced a positive in me. It was a negative for him but a positive for me. His negativity motivated me not to allow drinking to destroy my life.

But in the course of this life, the process of *forgetting, remembering, and reaching* is a combination of learning from both the good and the bad, balancing the negatives and positives. Learn to duplicate in your life the good you possess and see in others; reject the behavior of anyone in a negative or unhelpful way. Jesus's advice to Paul in Acts 9:5b is worth repeating for you and me: "***It is dangerous and it will turn out*** *badly for you to keep kicking against the goad [to offer vain and perilous resistance"]*. If you, for example, kick a barbed wire fence barefoot or punch it barehanded, it will be your foot or hand that will suffer, not the fence.

Had I not learned firsthand the dangers of alcoholism from my Dad, I might not have stopped drinking before it was too late. However, some family members seem destined, though I pray not, to be like Dad.

Chapter 8

Think It Not Strange

It is very important to learn how to remember to forget and receive. Sometimes, however, we are misled into believing that we are the only person in the history of the world to experience whatever it is we are dealing with. One of many possible reasons for adopting this flawed or religious type of belief is to assume everyone deals with trials and tribulations the same way. If you listen to Satan, who is a pathological liar, he will convince you that you are all alone, forgotten and forsaken by God, and that no one cares or understands what you are going through.

If the preceding beliefs are similar to what you think or have thought, listen to the apostle Peter, who was eventually martyred, who had his share of trials and tribulations. "Beloved, do not be amazed and bewildered at the fiery ordeal which is taking place to test your quality, as though something strange (unusual and alien to you and your position) were befalling you" (I Pet. 4:12). If the devil is not rocking your boat, check yourself to make sure you are not a beguiled passenger on his boat. Instead of expecting life to be without satanic attacks and challenges, be prepared to expect the unexpected; live watchfully and courageously with focused purpose. Do not allow your past to determine your present or predict your future. In this life, your lifelong journey will include coming out of a storm, living in or going through a storm, or heading into a storm. There will be peaks and valleys, ups and downs, temporary defeats and eternal victories.

The way you look at a situation determines how you deal with it. Take the game of basketball, for example, a few superstars say the secret to their success is their ability to stay in the moment during the game. In other words, they block out what did or didn't happen. The last game is not a prediction of the present game. Such a player understands yesterday was yesterday, and that today is today, all by itself. These superstars can forget about what was or was not, and focus on what is. They refuse to entertain thoughts that *this* game will be a repeat of the previous game. They play with the attitude that they can overcome past failures and surpass recent victories.

Listen! Forget yesterday's failures. Don't allow them to lord over today. Remember who you are in God and receive by faith the promises of God. Call those things that are not as though they were. Focus on the now. Don't look back. You may shipwreck your faith and fail to see what is right before you. But at the same time, don't try to look further ahead than your spiritual eyes can see. You may fail to see what you need to focus on and end up looking at what you did not and cannot see. As you look and press forward, look and press from where you are, not from where you wish you were.

Why Remember the Things You Want to Forget?

A good memory for the wrong reasons is a stumbling block, instead of a stepping-stone or a bridge across troubled waters. Be careful not to assume all challenges are warning signs that you are living in sin or not operating in the divine will of God. The called are chosen and are often placed by

God in difficult situations to lead His people out of. Take Jeremiah, for example, who was also known as the weeping prophet. Much of his suffering was not because of personal sins. It was the opposite. He was standing in the gap for his people.

By leaning and depending on God for strength and guidance, Jeremiah served the people by remembering His promises. ["O Lord] remember [earnestly] my affliction and my misery, my wandering *and* my outcast state, the wormwood and the gall" (Lam. 3:19). The gall is symbolic of suffering or judgment, the horrible taste of despair left in the mouth. By remembering God's faithfulness and compassion, Jeremiah was strengthened, able to look beyond his suffering to God for strength and guidance. Learn how to victoriously go through whatever it is you are going through. The things happening to you are not nearly as important as what is happening in and for you. The way you deal with trials and tribulations will definitely determine your outcome. So, are you fully persuaded the Lord is with, upon, and in you?

For example, look at the apostle Paul. He is, in many ways, a perfect example of what remembering is all about. He encouraged the saints at the Thessalonian church with these words in I Thessalonians 1:3,

"Recalling unceasingly before our God and Father your work energized by faith and service motivated by love and unwavering hope in [the return of] our Lord Jesus Christ (the Messiah"). [Compare I Thess. 1:10.] As you can see, remembering God's promises to you and others will endow you with the power not to focus so much on personal trials and tribulations. Keep in mind, remembering and forgetting include both negative and positive aspects of reaching. There are times when you must remember what needs to be forgotten and then forget it. At other times, you must choose to forget to remember past experiences to prevent them from lording over you. Forgetting to remember and remembering to forget instead of learning from past experiences. Part of the learning process includes leaving the negative aspects of your experiences in the past and reaching for the promises of God in the present.

To become or to remain bogged down in what happened in the past and refusing to remember the importance of forgetting is a type of imprisonment that will leave you stuck in the past. When this is allowed to happen, all hope and zeal for the future dwindles to a level of weariness. Could it be that people who commit suicide with installments of despair and hopelessness are either unable or unwilling to see how it is possible to overcome their trials, whether real or imagined? An effective way to look beyond what you see or can't see is not to overly focus on what you are looking at or for. Instead, remember whom you are looking to in the spirit realm and reach for the promises of God with all your heart, soul, and mind. In other words, press forward with every fiber of your being. Most important of all, if you have chosen to remember pain and disappointment, you could have chosen to forget the past and remember how blessed you are from the lessons learned. Also, you are made stronger by looking forward instead of growing increasingly weary from looking in the rearview mirror of life. So reach up to God and receive the blessings that await you. You are now, believe it or not, stronger than you have ever been, but not as strong as you are becoming. Allow Christ to strengthen you where you are weak.

Had Paul not learned the art of forgetting, he would not have been able to endure and serve the risen Christ. Saul the persecutor became Paul the persecuted! He shared some of his trials and tribulations in II Corinthians 11:23-27: "Are they [ministering] servants of Christ (the Messiah)? I am talking like one beside himself [but] I am more, with far more extensive and abundant labors, with far more imprisonments, [beaten] with countless stripes, and frequently [at the point] of death. Five times I received from [the hands of] the Jews forty [lashes all] but one; [Compare Deut. 25:3.] Three times I have been beaten with rods; once I was stoned. Three times I have been aboard a ship wrecked at sea; a [whole] night and a day I have spent [adrift] on the deep. Many times on journeys, [exposed to] perils from rivers, perils from bandits, perils from [my own] nation, perils from the Gentiles, perils in the city, perils in the desert places, perils in the sea, perils from those posing as believers [but destitute of Christian knowledge and piety]; In toil and hardship, watching often [through sleepless nights], in hunger and thirst, frequently driven to fasting by want, in cold and exposure and lack of clothing."

Let us be perfectly honest. Most of us have not and will not likely experience Paul's degree of suffering, but whether you will or not isn't the point. It is one thing to say what we will or will not do, but imagine the unimaginable suffering Paul endured. Most impressive of all, he never complained. He gloried in his suffering, preaching Christ, and Him crucified. However, it is easy and painless to sit back in an easy chair at home or on a pew in church and praise Paul for his faithfulness, though faithful he was! But praising Paul for his faithfulness will not change our lives unless we do what he did, fulfill our upward calling of God in Christ Jesus!

It is Receiving Time

Philippians 4:15 – And you Philippians yourselves well know that in the early days of the Gospel ministry, when **I** left Macedonia, no church (assembly) entered into partnership with me *and* opened up [a debit and credit] account in giving and receiving except you only.

Hebrews 12:28 – Let us therefore, receiving a kingdom that is firm *and* stable *and* cannot be shaken, offer to God pleasing service *and* acceptable worship, with modesty *and* pious care and godly fear *and* awe.

I Peter 1:9 – [At the same time] you receive the result (outcome,

consummation) of your faith, the
salvation of your souls.

Receiving salvation is an invitation. Receive the Holy Ghost is an invitation with a promise. Receiving your healing is also an invitation. Receiving forgiveness is also an invitation. Everything God has for us is ours by invitation. The key, if you will, to receiving is forgetting and remembering. Forget your defeats and victories. Always remember yesterday's failures and triumphs belong to the past. Receive today as the new day that it is, full of new grace, mercy, and divine promises. In the words of Leslie Poles Hartley, "The past is a foreign country; they do things differently there." – SWEETWATER PRESS, What They Said, p. 602. Focus on what's good, and the good you can do. Bishop Mant said, "That which is good to be done, cannot be done too soon; and if it is neglected to be done early, it will frequently happen that it will not be done at all." – Webster's Encyclopedia of Dictionaries, New American Edition, p. 877.

Anyone who refuses to forget to remember and reach is in danger of being lured into waiting and waiting until it's too late to do anything.

What Does Love Have to Do with *Forgetting, Remembering, and Reaching?*

What does love have to do with it? Everything! The ability, willingness, and enablement to forget, remember, and reach depend on your capacity to love, and love opens the doorway to forgiveness. Moreover, the willingness to forgive is achieved by developing a negative memory, a choice not to harbor hurt or plot revenge. A negative memory is the ability to remember a wrong suffered without allowing it to dictate how you treat that person. Any memory of a wrong committed against you should be used to build, not to tear down.

Read and Do Something

Anyone who has read or at least thumbed through the Bible may have read I Corinthians 13, often referred to as the love chapter. It is worthy of that distinction, but the entire Bible is a love letter, though it also warns us of the consequences of rejecting God's love. In John 3:16 Jesus tells us, "For God so greatly loved and dearly prized the world that He [even] gave up His only begotten (unique) Son, so that whoever believes in (trusts in, clings to, relies on)

Him shall not perish (come to destruction, be lost) but have eternal (everlasting) life." Proverbs 10:12 and I Peter 4:8 have this to say about love: "Hatred stirs up contentions, but love covers all transgressions. Above all things have intense and unfailing love for one another, for love covers a multitude of sins [forgives and disregards the offenses of others"].

Arguably, everything wrong in the world today is, more often than not, because unloving and powerful people are seemingly determined to control the lives of everyone else. However, the apostle John shares the following truths recorded in I John 3:15 & 4:18=21, "Anyone who hates (abominates, detests) his brother [in Christ] is [at heart] a murderer, and you know that no murderer has eternal life abiding (persevering) within him. There is no fear in love [dread does not exist], but full–grown (complete, perfect) love turns fear out of doors and expels every trace of terror! For fear brings with it the thought of punishment, and [so] he who is afraid has not reached the full maturity of love [is not yet grown into love's complete perfection]. We love Him, because He first loved us. If anyone says, I love God, and hates (detests, abominates) his brother [in Christ], he is a liar; for he who does not love his brother, whom he has seen, cannot love God, Whom he has not seen.

And this command (charge, order, injunction) we have from Him: that he who loves God shall love his brother [believer] also."

The number of murders committed every day is tragically becoming an epidemic norm. However, if it's not a family member or close friend murdered, most of us tend to hear, but not hear. Yet most of us need to know that God compares hate to that of murder. It is understandable that physically killing someone causes more pain and grief than hating him or her, though oftentimes hate leads to murder. Nonetheless, God likens a believer hating a believer to that of a murderer, and although everyone is not a believer, it is up to believers to be an example to unbelievers by loving one another. The point to glean from this narrative is that hating one another will no more go unpunished than murder. Most important of all, do not forget to remember that the person you love the least is the most you love God. So, how much or little do you love God? This question demands an answer!

Forgetting, Remembering, and Reaching in Real Time

Real time, as you know, is the actual time during which something takes place. Given the term is used several times in this book, it seems fitting and proper to say a little more about *real time* to ensure you relate it to what it means within the context of this book. *Real time* is a continuous presence where there is either action or inaction taking place, and is an important part of *forgetting, remembering, and reaching*. But *forgetting, remembering, and reaching* is not only something we do when it is convenient or serves a selfish purpose; it is what we should do. Remember, if you are not doing something important, unimportant nothings will be held onto that should have been released, which will cause something important to be lost that could have been gained. Real time is happening now, always now. It is not was, or will be. It is now!

Furthermore, the way we handle physical, mental, emotional pain, and stress has a lot to do with how we deal with *forgetting, remembering, and reaching*. For instance, during a family gathering, some of the women jokingly but seriously reminded the men that we don't know anything about pain, because we don't know how it feels to have a baby. And that's the truth. Therefore we couldn't defend ourselves regarding that particular point.

However, the severity of pain is usually rated on a scale of 1 to 10, but that's not an exact science. One person will likely rate his or her pain differently from that of someone else. A rating of 5 for your pain may be higher or lower for someone else's, or vice versa. But on a personal note, I have a high pain tolerance. But of course, I reached this conclusion by self-rating my tolerance for pain based on personal experiences.

Case in point. When in high school, I crashed into the corner wing of a building playing football and fractured a bone in my left wrist. I ignored the pain and attended classes for the rest of the day. But when changing classes, a friend, who was unaware of my injury, caught up with me in the crowded hallway and yanked on my arm from behind. What would have likely been a painless gesture under normal conditions, sent shock-wave pains throughout my entire body! I quickly dropped to my knees to ease the agonizing pain.

My wrist was fitted with a cast up to the elbow. The doctor warned Mom that my left wrist might be permanently paralyzed because the fracture was in a delicate place that might stop the flow of blood after it healed. But being a typical tenth-grader, during which time young people weren't killing each other like flies, and since we believed only old folks got sick or died, thinking my left wrist would be paralyzed never really crossed my mind.

My arm was in a cast for three months. After a week or so, I learned how to use that cask as a defensive weapon when playing football. It came in handy for blocking, and I quickly mastered catching the ball with one hand better than everyone with two hands could. Sometimes we played games on the school campus, and at other times in the street where we lived. Whenever the football hit the power lines and knocked off the electricity, we would run for cover. Neither our parents nor the neighbors paid very much attention to the temporary power outages. Anyway, I fell on the concrete playing football two days after the cast was removed. Thank God the fall didn't cause any problems for my wrist or any other body parts.

But getting back to the matter of pain. I can't possibly compare the pain I've experienced with that of a woman having a baby. Yet if I were to try, I can't imagine having a baby is more painful than that of my fractured wrist. Nevertheless, it is unwise to assume the way you or I handle pain will be the same for everyone else. At any rate, the fracture was my first experience with extreme piercing pain.

The next encounter with pain surpassed that of my fractured wrist occurred, figuratively speaking, a lifetime later in 2016. It was a humid overcast on a mid-September afternoon. It was unclear whether it was an ideal time to clear the weeds from the long downhill driveway. Because rain was in the forecast, I loaded the Weed Eater and some other equipment in our SUV and backed down the driveway to the worksite. Sure enough, it began to rain. With the Weed Eater in hand with the strap over my neck and shoulder, I turned carefully and slowly to walk to the vehicle. Seemingly, some supernatural force swooped down and knocked me off my feet, hurled me high into midair, and slammed–dunked me onto the asphalt on my left hip. Yes! Based on the unusual way the fall occurred, I am fully convinced it was a demonic attack. I cried out silently without giving voice to the piercing pain, yet I managed to utter, "Oh my God!" The intensity of the pain was a first for me. If having a baby is more painful, I humbly apologize to every mother and expecting mother in the entire world.

The pain numbed my senses to the point that I acted instinctively rather than deliberately, if that makes any sense. Had I cried out for help, no one was within earshot of me, so "Oh my God" was my cry for help. With each carefully placed step, the pain shot from my hip throughout my entire body. I hobbled to the SUV, loaded the tools, drove to the house, limped into the house toward the bedroom, using furnishings and walls to steady my pained walk to the shower. Afterward, I called my wife at work, told her I had fallen, and "I think I may need to go to the hospital." I am so grateful God led me to drive the SUV. Otherwise, I don't believe I would have been able to walk uphill to our home.

While waiting for my wife, I also managed to slip on clothes suitable for an emergency room visit. More than two hours, plus a painful eternity, passed between falling and getting to the hospital, and three more hours passed before the examination process began. On one hand, it may have been less than three hours, but in the pain time zone, it was at least three hours for sure! But on the other hand, I understood emergency rooms function as triages, and the most critically ill patients are treated first, but knowing that did not ease the pain. So shortly before forever, X-rays were taken, and the diagnosis was a broken hip, surgery, partial hip replacement, and weeks of therapy to follow.

Physical therapy included various types of exercises typical for my injury. I quickly graduated from using a walker to a cane. Perhaps most important of all, l learned a life-changing lesson that had little to do with my hip, but it was learned as a result of having broken my hip. The therapist warned me not to favor my left hip because I would develop a limp that would likely become permanent after rehab. To avoid limping, I purposefully practiced the art of *forgetting, remembering, and reaching*. The process involved forgetting the fall, the pain, and being fully persuaded that I would walk without a limp after rehabilitation. I had to also forget about the experience, or the possible physical problems that a broken hip could cause after the fact. I had to remember to do the exercises properly, practice walking without limping, although it caused extreme pain, not to favor the injured hip. I had to reach for and expect to fully recover, trusting God to do for me what I couldn't do, heal myself.

For several months, I had to use my hands and arms to stand from a sitting position. After I was healed and regained my strength, I continued, though unnecessarily, to use my hands and arms to help lift myself from a sitting to a standing position. It was a struggle breaking a practice that was now an unnecessary habit. I had to unlearn doing out of habit what I had learned to do out of necessity. Finally, I stopped using my hands or overthinking the process. I could now stand up without using my hands, but it was still difficult to resist using them. *Forgetting, remembering, and reaching* helped me to unlearn a practice that was now an unneeded habit.

It was expedient for me to forget what I had learned but no longer needed, and remember I was healed and reach for or proclaim my healing by trusting my legs. Point being, life can become a crippling experience if you ignore the importance of *forgetting, remembering, and reaching*. It is needful to understand that forgetting represents letting go of the past, remembering the present, and reaching or pressing toward future possibilities. Keep also in mind that if you develop a limp in your spiritual walk, and try to avoid the pains of trials and tribulations by giving in to them, you will cripple your spiritual walk. It takes effort and determination to unlearn a feeble spiritual walk that should not have been learned and practiced in the first place.

Pain is Deceptive and Personal

Never dismiss what a person is feeling as imaginary, unimportant, or exaggerated. Instead, be sympathetic and understand that the two of you are different people. Listen and remember that the threshold for pain is not the same for everyone. For example, men and women who were prisoners or victims of war suffered pain and cruelty beyond what most of us can even imagine. Their capacity to endure pain and suffering was beyond that of having a tolerance for bearing the severest kind of pain that most of us are unfamiliar with. It was a matter of finding peace, strength, and forgiveness to endure pain and suffering by resting in the arms of Jesus and forgiving their persecutors who were inflicting them with unimaginable pain and suffering. Regardless, it's a waste of time debating who can handle the most pain. Resist the temptation of assuming you know the extent of someone else's pain. Instead, comfort the comfortless and pray that they will be able to endure. Never ever tell anyone his or her pain is a mere invention of the mind.

Sometimes it is necessary to forget what you think about a person and remember he or she is a unique person who deserves to live a meaningful and fulfilling life. And although you may believe you are treating people right, in the eyes of God, you might be unloving and judgmental. You may also believe the way you are treating a person is right because you were treated the same way in the past. This is why forgetting is so important. We are told in I Thessalonians 5:15, "See that none of you repays another with evil for evil, but always aim to show kindness and seek to do good to one another and to everybody." To obey this scripture, you need to read, study, remember, and practice it. Rely on the Holy Spirit to bring to your remembrance everything Jesus is saying to you in the Bible. It is the Holy Spirit who gives you the power to forget, remember, and reach. It is not you. Otherwise, you would likely brag and boast.

Chapter 9

The Bible is a Love Letter

Allow me to share with you *my* scientific method for deciding whether or not to buy a particular book. Please note I am not saying this method is scientific, but that it is *my* scientific method. It is of course, helpful if something is known about the author's character and previous books, if any. In any event, I'll read the book's beginning and ending pages. The way it begins and ends says a lot about what happens between the beginning and the ending.

The next step, the book between the palms of my hands, with the thumbs resting on the edges of the cover, is opened to a random page, and the first words my eyes focus on are read. If that page captures my attention, the process is repeated several times, and the words my eyes are drawn to on a randomly selected page are a sign to buy the book. Finally, *my* scientific investigation may lead to reading the table of contents and the introduction. If *my* attention continues to be captured during this process, purchasing the book is the next step.

Although the previous suggestions are among my helpful ways to shop for a book, having an intimate relationship with its author is even better. Therefore, purchasing a Bible is an easy decision to make. But when it comes to studying the Bible, my approach is totally different. First of all, I am very familiar with the author, the Holy Spirit. Even so, choosing the right Bible translation is not always an easy decision. After the purchase is made, it is not always easy to decide where to begin studying. This is especially true for new converts. There are, of course, many teaching tools to help direct one's study. One of many suggestions is to begin studying Scriptures that will teach you how to deal with whatever it is you are dealing with or going through at that particular time. Regardless, the most important thing is to get started, or to develop daily study habits if you have already begun.

If you are in a hurry or have a pressing need to understand God's plans and purposes for your life, read the beginning and the ending of God's love letter written to and about you. Read what happened in the beginning in Genesis and the conclusion in the last chapter of Revelation. Or the Holy Spirit may lead you to particular verses that will show you how much God loves you. In any event, understand that the Bible is much more than the Word of God written to people in general. It is a love letter written by God to you in particular. God had you in mind when He created you. You are not a random person or a meaningless number in the crowd of humanity. God is watching over you in the crowd!

God's love letter to you includes humanity through every epoch of history. The life God created for Adam and Eve, He is restoring by making everything new in the last chapter of Revelation. Moreover, the theme, if you will, throughout the Bible is that God loves you so very much. Everything the first Adam forfeited, the last Adam, Christ, will make new! But had God not made a way for us through Christ Jesus to reconcile us to Himself, we would not be able to experience the love of God in our lives.

But an unread book, regardless of its contents, cannot help you any more than uncooked food in the freezer can fill your hunger. Also, you need to study the Word of God, but it will not change anything in your life unless you are willing to obey and give your life back to the Giver of life. You must allow God to deliver you from the life you inherited and lived before you surrendered to Christ. However, even after God delivers you, ask Him to teach you how to walk in your deliverance that starts and continues by *forgetting, remembering, and reaching.*

Yet everything that has or will be shared in this book regarding *forgetting, remembering, and reaching* is only the beginning; the discipline to perfect this process is a lifelong pursuit that should be practiced daily. Therefore, not too much can be said about its importance. At the same time, always remember Jesus identifies Himself as the Truth, and the devil as the father of lies. But don't focus on the lies of the liar; remember and reach for the promises of redemption and eternal life through Christ Jesus.

Keys to Forgetting What You Are Remembering

You can remember not to forget or you can forget to remember and reach. In other words, it is as important to remember what to forget as it is to forget to remember things that are forgotten. You can choose not to forgive and hold people hostage by not forgetting. The key to forgetting hurts and disappointments is accomplished by remembering and sharing the power of love. Love heals the heart of pain and wrongs suffered. Love is stronger than any hurt or disappointment you may be nursing that is holding onto you. So, each time you are tempted to be unforgiving, forgive! Each time you consider hating, love! Each time you are tempted to remember what was not, remember what is! And each time you are tempted to gossip, speak the truth.

However, keep in mind that there are both positive and negative aspects to remembering. Commit to forgetting things that are wrong and spiritually unhealthy. Commit to remembering what and who is right. The discipline to remember what God is saying, and forgetting what the devil is saying and plotting, takes practice. Nevertheless, learn to forgive, erase, reclaim, embrace, proclaim, and hide the promises of God in your heart.

Forgetting can be likened to a chalkboard that is arguably being used less and less in the classroom. You can write and erase on a chalkboard without damaging or changing it. When you truly forgive, the negative aspects of memory are rendered powerless by the heart, though the mind retains them as a matter of fact from which wisdom and knowledge are derived. The heart is safeguarded from hate and revenge when committed to forgiving, remembering, and reaching. The heart will then welcome each day afresh and will see people through the eyes of God. Refuse to look at people based on where they were or what they did. Ask God to help you see people as He does.

Think about, for example, the marriage that can be restored if the couple is willing to clean the slate, erase the chalkboard, so to speak, and begin anew with a renewed commitment of love and reconciliation. The reason so much is wrong and lacking in the world, and consequently in our lives, is that love and selflessness have been uprooted by hate, indifference, and selfishness. Wherever love is lacking, chaos reigns. Love begins and spreads from the family nucleus. But when love is lacking in the family, hate is ignited, burns like wildfire, and consumes lives along its destructive path.

Each of us needs to read, reread, set aside quality time for prayerful study, and learn to live and manifest the essence of God's love letter. We can learn to love God and others with His love. What the world needs now is love!!! Love for God and fellowman, instead of love of wealth and power, for the sake of wealth and power.

Living in the Present, Out of the Past, into the Future

> **II Corinthians 5:17** – Therefore if any person is [ingrafted] in Christ (the Messiah) he is a new creation (a new creature altogether); the old [previous moral and spiritual condition] has passed away. Behold, the fresh *and* new has come!

> Even God cannot change the past – AGATHON (448-400 BC). *What They Said,* The Ultimate Authoritative Book of Quotations, p. 128.

> Nothing endures but change – HERACLITUS (C. 535-475 BC). *What They Said,* The Ultimate Authoritative Book of Quotations, p. 129.

Every word, jot, and tittle in every verse of the Bible is a vital part of the Word of God, whether we believe it or understand it or not. Although this is true, attention is being directed to several words in the previous verse that stress the importance of living in the now. Do not forget to remember that everything that happens or does not happen, that is done or not done, said or not said, always takes place in the present and moves forward into the awaiting arms of the future.

Let's reread 2 Corinthians 5:17 (KJV) "Therefore if any man be in Christ, he is a new creature: old things are passed away; behold; behold, all things are become new."

Take a closer look at the following words:

1. Be – To be in Christ is to have a relationship with Him by virtue of the new birth
2. Is – Present tense is your reality or position in Christ
3. New – A new creature in Christ, continually being renewed, growing, and maturing in Him
4. Passed – The past is past. It no longer exists in the present.
5. Are – Your present position in God

6. Things – past behavior and lifestyle were, but no longer are
7. Become – The person you are is a foregone transformation, a continual present conclusion

Your relationship with Christ is a constant manifestation in the now. The reason God doesn't, rather *can't,* change the past is that when it was the present, He did everything exactly the way He desired to. However, to even suggest God needs to change the past would imply He didn't get it right in the first place, which is, of course, untrue! But each of us must change for the change. In a metaphoric sense, the only constant in life is change, and it takes place in us as we worship God, who is unchanging.

You Can Look Back, but You Can't Go Back

An instruction booklet or manual is provided with new merchandise to help the buyer assemble and operate the product. The manual is also helpful when troubleshooting problems. If a product is not working properly, referring to the instruction manual is one of the best ways to begin the troubleshooting process. On the other hand, when a defect in a product is identified or discovered, the manufacturer will, if possible, fix or correct it. The company will not likely ignore or stubbornly refuse to correct problems or defects that are in the best interest of the manufacturer and the consumer. Thank God, the products made by man can be improved to be better and safer. And the safety of a product should always be more important than sales and profit. Of course, safety records and the manufacturer's commitment to invest in research and development will ensure the production of better and safer products. Point being, if the product is faulty, so is the instruction booklet or manual. As a result, there are, for example, frequent recalls and updates, and the replacement of defective parts on cars and many other products.

Unlike manmade products, the Bible, the Word of God, is inerrant and not in need of recalls and updates. It is as up-to-date, as holy, and as relevant today as it was when, in Genesis 1:3, God's utterance began a series of proclamations, "Let there be..." This truth is particularly important when it comes to the Word of God. We must learn to "let there be" that which is. To get the most out of life and living, let go of the past and live in the present. Not only can you not retrieve the past, but any attempt to do so will cause you to ignore the present. Sadly, will likely forget to embrace the future that is being birthed from within the passing moments of the present. When we live life in the present and obey the Word of God, it sets us free from the snares of the past, free to live, reach, and prepare for the future that is the offspring of the present. Most important of all, the Bible instructs and teaches us how to present our vessels honorably by living the way God created us to. So, before you try to adapt and understand life according to the will of God, read and study your *Operational Manual,* the Holy Bible. You can also use the Bible to troubleshoot your shortcomings.

Forget to Remember

The following personal experiences illustrate the importance of *forgetting, remembering, and reaching,* to include how to forget to remember, and how to remember to forget: Joining the US Army after high school was my first extended stay away from home. After Basic Training and a two-week leave back home, Advanced Infantry Training (AIT) began. For the first several weeks of AIT, I awoke each morning at reveille thinking I was at home. This unsettling awakening from a dreamlike illusion, nightmare, or whatever it was, left me confused and conflicted for a few seconds. After looking around and hearing the roaring and screaming voices of the sergeants, I was quickly shaken back to reality.

Following AIT, I was shipped to Germany and was there for almost three years until my Expiration Term of Service (ETS). As my ETS date neared, I began to think about friends and the life I left behind three years ago. I flew from Frankfurt, Germany, to New Orleans, Louisiana, to pick up my new Ford Mustang that I had been paying on for about a year. It was a beast of a muscle car, specially ordered with a powerful engine and every hotrod type option available from the factory. But I didn't have a job, so the dealership wouldn't finance it. Instead, they approved financing for a Mustang much tamer and cheaper than the beast, especially ordered for my hot-rodding delight. I was naturally disappointed but accepted a scaled-down version of my dream car. Anyway, the finance manager called my former employer, who hired me on the spot and told me to return to work the following week.

But before I left Germany, I began to look forward to returning home to the life I left behind three years ago. But to my surprise, everything had changed! The city had changed. It didn't even look the same, and

I didn't see it the same. My old friends had changed. Some were in college, married, or relocated. I felt out of place. I suddenly realized, *back* is not *back* there. It left when I left. I had forgotten to remember by not remembering to forget. I forgot to remember that what I left when joining the Army was not what I was returning to. Again, since I forgot to remember, I did not remember to forget. Although this sounds like double talk, it is a matter of identifying conflicting emotions twisted together by unrealistic memories that need to be worked through.

Chapter 10

God Said and God Did

Genesis 1:24, 25 – And God said, Let the earth bring forth living creatures according to their kinds: livestock, creeping things, and [wild] beasts of the earth according to their kinds. And it was so. And God made the [wild] beasts of the earth according to their kinds, and domestic animals according to their kinds, and everything that creeps upon the earth according to its kind. And God saw that it was good (fitting, pleasant) *and* He approved it.

The best way to understand what we should be doing is to go back to the beginning of creation when God set everything in order according to His divine will. What God created or made in verse 25 is He said He would make in verse 24. Not only that, God commanded every creature to reproduce after its kind. Cattle reproduce cattle, goats reproduce goats, ants reproduce ants, and so forth. In a word, God said and God did. His creation did as God said.

When I was *MUCH* younger, life was simpler: black and white, not a reference to race, was clearly defined and easily identifiable. Right and wrong, even when the fiber of morality was violated, the holiness of God was not degraded and dishonored by unethical lifestyles. At least sins that were once an ignited spark are now an out-of-control wildfire. We are out of order when we try to undo or redo what God did. Only humanity has created disorder out of order and created gender confusion. Each of us has the power of choice to obey or to disobey God, and to do our own thing, whatever it may be. But time, as we know it, is running out of time, and eternity is close at hand. The decisions we are making will determine where we spend eternity. In other words, judgment day is coming.

Now, back to the matter of everything reproducing after its kind: two male beasts will fight for the rights to mate with a female beast of their kind, but they will never fight to mate with each other. All of God's creation does what it does naturally and according to God's created plan. Only human beings have the power of choice and are therefore capable of acting in ways contrary to nature and the will of God. And although God teaches us what the right choices are, He does not take away our power to choose, be it right or wrong, good or evil, holy or unholy, whether it produces life or death. There is a divine order set forth by God that we are commanded to obey. God does not force us to obey Him. That has not, and will not, change!

> **Genesis 1:26, 27** – God said, Let Us [Father, Son, and Holy Spirit] make mankind is Our image, after Our likeness, and let them have complete authority over the fish of the sea, the birds of the air, the [tame] beasts, and over all of the earth, and over everything that creeps upon the earth. [Compare Ps, 104:30; Heb.

1:2; 11:3.] So God created man in His own image, in the image *and* likeness of God He created him; male and female He created them. [Compare Col. 3:9, 10: James 3:8, 9.]

In verse 26, God said, Let Us make man in Our image, after Our likeness, and in verse 27, God created man exactly the way He said He would make or create him, male and female. God cannot lie. He said what He was going to do before He did it. We are made in the image and likeness of God. We are created to emulate God's character. If committed to obeying the truth, we will say and then do. We can learn, among other lessons, the creative power of the tongue and that we will possess what we confess.

The tongue is a dangerous member of the body in the mouth of an unlearned, unrighteous, unloving, or undisciplined person! Proverbs 18:21 explains it with unmistakable clarity: "Death and life are in the power of the tongue, and they who indulge in it shall eat the fruit of it [for death or life"]. The tongue is the conveyor of life and death, so think about what you going to say before you say it.

Genesis 1:28 – And God blessed them and said to them, Be fruitful, multiply, and fill the earth, and subdue it [using all its vast resources in the service of God and man]; and have dominion over the fish of the sea, the birds of the air, and over every living creature that moves upon the earth.

God created Adam and Eve and gave them a mandate that has not changed. We have authority over everything in the sea, in the air, and on the earth. We are commanded to subdue or to master the earth with dominion above, on, and beneath the earth. God has given mankind unrivalled authority over His creation. God did not tell us that we have dominion over each other. He created us to have dominion over things, not each other.

His instructions concerning our relationship with Him and each other are made clear in Matthew 22:37-40, "And He replied to him, You shall love the Lord your God with all your heart and with all your soul and with all your mind (intellect). [Compare Deut. 6:5.] This is the great (most important, principal) and first commandment. And a second is like it: You shall love your neighbor as [you do] yourself. [Compare Lev. 19:18.] These two commandments are the sum total of all the Law and the Prophets."

Loving God with all the heart, soul, and mind is total love for God, and no part of self is withheld. Our love for God empowers and commands us to love each other. When we love God with all of our heart, soul, and mind, the temptation to lord or rule over each other is eliminated. If mankind obeys these two commandments, most of everything that is wrong in the entire world would begin to disappear overnight. Far too many of us have modified how we obey God and the laws of the land. It is easy to obey the commandments and laws that you agree with, or that do not require you to make changes and sacrifices. It is much easier to disobey when change and obedience are required.

We must avoid being like the Pharisees and Sadducees, whom Jesus often described as hypocrites and vipers, fools and blind. In Matthew 23:24, He levies a very serious charge against them, "You blind guides, filtering out a gnat and gulping down a camel!" [Compare Lev. 27:30; Mic. 6:8.] Jesus accused them of nitpicking over minor issues and ignoring the most important matters. A fitting metaphor is making a mountain out of a mole, or looking at an ant-sized situation as if it's an elephant-sized problem. In other words, majoring in minors and minoring in majors is to give the least important issues the most attention, and the most important issues little or no attention. This falls miserably short of obeying God and allowing love to shape, control, and direct how we treat each other.

A Spiritual Exodus from Your Egypt

Jesus shared two infallible truths in John 14:2 and Mark 3:25, "In My Father's house there are many dwelling places (homes). If it were not so, I would have told you; for I am going away to prepare a place for you. And if a house is divided (split into factions and rebelling) against itself, that house will not be able to last." But prior to this verse, Jesus also said in Mark 3:24, "And if a kingdom is divided and rebelling against itself, that kingdom cannot stand." Interestingly, the meaning of the word house in John 14:2 and Mark 3:25 is the same.

A brief look at history is a stern reminder of the tragedies of divided houses and kingdoms. There were North and South Vietnam, one people with different political philosophies. There was an East and West Germany, one people separated by different forms of government. There's a North and South Korea, one people with opposing political views. There was a North and South United States of America, one people with warring views on slavery and equal rights that led to war and bloodshed. There is a racial and economic divide in America. There is the Red and Blue, one people whose political parties are seemingly more important than the people whom they are elected to serve.

Consequently, the soul of democracy is under a vicious attack. There is, in my opinion, very little substantive difference between the parties. Individuals from within each party step out, from time to time, from the shadows of obscurity and go against the political grain of their party by supporting sweeping changes amid chaos. America is a rainbow nation of people who are becoming increasingly separated across the racial, political, and financial divide. But any civilized nation fighting and warring from within is terminally ill with political, social, and economic *cancer* that spreads and metastasizes in the hearts, minds, and souls of the people. A divided house cannot stand, survive, or prosper.

Let us not forget about the Trojan horse, defined by *Merriam-Webster's Deluxe Dictionary* as "someone or something intended to defeat or subvert from within, usually by means of deception."

Family in Heaven, Enemies in Hell

Allow me to appeal to you who believe heaven and hell are real places. Also, every believer is part of the family of God, whose focus and affections should be heavenward. Everyone who ends up in hell is an enemy of God, though God loves everyone, whether they love Him or not. The reality of heaven and hell is not proved or disproved based on whether or not you believe. What you believe or disbelieve does not change the truth. If you don't believe heaven and hell are real, I suggest you skip over this section and go to the next topic. But for those who do believe, don't forget to remember that heaven and hell will include some of everybody. We should learn to love everyone in this life, because whether we love him or her or not will have everything to do with where and with whom we spend eternity. If you don't learn to love here on earth, you will spend eternity in hell with everybody you hated on earth. Love is your passport to heaven, and your visa is stamped with *forgetting, remembering, and reaching.*

Do You Love Me More than These?

The word love, like most words, has more than one meaning. It is probably the most abused and misused word in any language. Most of our first encounters with the word love are derived from the way it is mostly used outside of a Christian setting. It is used to express feelings and opinions about almost everything. We love movies, music, and dogs. We love the shoes and the clothes we wear. We love swimming, bicycling, basketball, and sports in general. We love so many things that it becomes difficult to tell what it is we love, or what we mean when we say we love.

Some people love hating, killing, cursing, and abusing young and innocent children. Some people love pornography, human slavery, and bondage. The word is used in every imaginable way. Some people love sex and having babies, many of whom are little more than babies themselves, who know as much about childrearing as they do about life on the moon. The word love is used so casually and freely that its true meanings have been lost or tossed aside in translation.

Peter had to learn the purest meaning of love when Jesus asked him, "Do you love me more than these?" After Jesus's arrest and crucifixion, Peter and the disciples, who were fishermen by trade, returned to doing what they were doing before they met Jesus, fishing. If you stop following Jesus, you will likely return to your old lifestyle. Jesus's question was puzzling and confusing to Peter.

The scriptures do not say what *these* are. *These* seem too impersonal and uncharacteristic for Jesus to have been referring to the other disciples or people in general. So, even if Jesus were talking about the disciples, it is doubtful that *these* are limited to only the disciples. *These* are plural for this, so perhaps Jesus was talking about anything and everything that could usurp or replace our love for Him. Or, maybe Jesus was pointing to the fish He had cooked for them when He asked the question. Also, the scriptures do not reveal how Jesus caught the fish. He may have caught them supernaturally while Peter and the other disciples were fishing themselves. Whether or not *these* refer to *people,* it probably includes anything and anyone that is loved more than or instead of Jesus Himself.

For you and me, *more than these* also include anything and everything more important to us than

Jesus. Whatever you claim to love that is drawing you away from serving Jesus is part of *these*. Peter, to repeat, had returned to fishing, which may have given him and the other disciples' dispirited hearts temporary relief from thinking about the death of Jesus. So, Jesus asked Peter the same question three times, and with a clear command for him to answer. Jesus wanted Peter to get a clear understanding of agape love to redirect his attention away from *these*, fishing, or whatever, by becoming fishers of men.

Before discussing the in-depth conversation between Jesus and Peter, take a closer look at the meaning(s) of the word *love*. A word can be used in different ways, so the setting or context in which it is used is very important. For example, when someone confesses their love for you, especially in a romantic way, make sure their definition of love is the same as yours. The person may love your eyes, hair, the way you walk, your physical appearance, and not necessarily the *real* you.

Personal experiences and relationships are largely responsible for how each of us forms our opinions of love. However, the meanings we attach to words do not necessarily express their true meaning. The way a person uses the word *love* may not have anything to do with love. In a word, love means different things to different people, depending on their understanding, or lack of, regarding love and matters of the heart.

Make sure you know what you are saying when you say *I love you,* and know what is meant when you are told, "I love you." Given that love means different things to different people, let us look at three ways love is used in the Scriptures. The Hebrew word *Ahab* includes loving God, friends, or it can refer to romantic interests. It also represents the thought of loving, to include love for certain principles, and numerous other things in a general sense of speaking. On the other hand, *phileo* love is to be particularly fond of a person, to cherish, or to have a strong personal attachment to. *Agape* love is volitional or an act of the will. It is sacrificial and self-giving. *Agape* love is the love God has for us, and the love we should have for Him and each other.

Love is very powerful. Be very careful not to use the word in an untruthful, deceptive, improper, or unloving way. One thing particularly puzzling about saying or believing the words, *I love you,* is that both honest and dishonest people use these three powerful words. A person who has been deceived, abused, or hurt by someone who said, *I love you,* might become gun-shy and reject a person who does love him or her. Consequently, harboring hurt and disappointment from the past may cause you to reject the affections of someone who loves you. However, the power and reliability of words do not depend so much on the words used, but on the character of the person using them. Always remember this truth: a person cannot give you that which he or she does not have. In order not to become or to remain scarred and distrustful because of past experiences, *forgetting, remembering, and reaching* are necessary steps en route to forgiveness and healing.

It is also understandable that most of us are probably unable to fully grasp the depth and unfailing power of love. We can start by drawing closer to the *God of love* to experience the *love of God*. The following conversation between Jesus and Peter will help us to better understand the meaning of love from God's point of view.

John 21:15-17 – When they had eaten, Jesus said to Simon Peter, Simon, son of John, do you love Me more than these [others do—with reasoning, intentional, spiritual devotion, as one loves the Father]? He said to Him, Yes, Lord, You know that **I** love You [that **I** have deep, instinctive, personal affection for You, as for a close friend]. He said to him, Feed My lambs. Again He said to him the second time, Simon, son of John, do you love Me [with reasoning, intentional, spiritual devotion, as one loves the Father]? He said to Him, Yes, Lord. You know that **I** love You [that **I** have a deep, instinctive, personal affection for You, as for a close friend]. He said to him, Shepherd (tend) My sheep. He said to him the third time, Simon, son of John, do you love Me [with a deep, instinctive, personal affection for Me, as for a close friend]? Peter was grieved (was saddened and was hurt) that He should ask him the third time, Do you love Me? And he said to Him, Lord, You know everything; You know that **I** love You [that **I** have a deep, instinctive, personal affection for

You, as for a close friend]. Jesus
said to him, Feed My sheep.

After Jesus was arrested, Peter denied knowing Him three times and his third denial was uttered with anger and cursing. Therefore, Jesus asked him three times if he loved Him more than *these?* Keep in mind, when Jesus questions or mentions *something* you did, His purpose is not to discourage you, but to help you turn a past failure into a present or future victory. The first two times Jesus questioned Peter, He was referring to *agape* love, but Peter answered Him all three times with *phileo* love, the only love he possessed and understood at that time. The third time Jesus questioned Peter, His reference was *phileo* love because that was all Peter knew.

Notice the difference between Jesus's questions and Peter's answers. Jesus asked, "Do you love me with reasoning, intentional, spiritual devotion, as one loves the Father?" Peter answered, "You know I have deep, instinctive, personal affection for You, as for a close friend." Jesus was questioning and commissioning Peter at the same time. Feed my lambs or the young believer was stressed once, and twice He stressed sheep or mature believers. In other words, Jesus was commissioning Peter to feed and nurture the body of Christ. After the day of Pentecost, the Holy Spirit empowered Peter with *agape* love, which he expounded on in his writings and personified in his ministry. To reiterate, if you do not love and follow Jesus, you will likely return to your old life in some shape, form, or fashion.

The importance of the conversation between Jesus and Peter cannot be overemphasized. Each engaged in a conversation about love with different meanings in mind. Peter's understanding of love was clear to him, which is the reason Jesus's question was repeated three times, though confusing and discouraging to Peter. Although Jesus understood Peter's answers, Peter needed to understand Jesus's questions.

To reiterate, Jesus asked Peter the first two times if he loved Him as one loves the Father. Peter confessed he loved Him as a close friend each time he was questioned. The third time, Jesus asked Peter if he loved Him as a close friend. Peter acknowledged Jesus knows everything, that he indeed loves Jesus as a close friend.

This is a perfect example of what happens when people apply different meanings to a word, thought, or question that needs to be clearly understood and answered. Jesus understood Peter, but Peter neither fully understood Jesus nor himself. Imagine what happens when neither a person nor a group of people understands each other. The consequences range from minor to major. The lack of like-mindedness is the main reason for the breakdown in communication and the demise of relationships. Unlike Jesus who understood Peter, the lack of mutual understanding or an unwillingness to communicate is responsible for untold pain and suffering.

Love is as Love Does

The importance of *forgetting, remembering, and reaching* has been discussed numerous times in various ways. And yet much more needs to be said, given most unbelievers, and some believers struggle with not living in the now presence of God. The unbelievers' problem is that they have not accepted Jesus as their personal Savior and therefore have no basis for trusting Him. Some believers have not yet learned to trust Him as Lord and Savior. If you are willing to let go and let God, Jesus will deliver and transform you.

Certain words Jesus spoke on the cross, under the most painful conditions, illustrate the power of *forgetting, remembering, and reaching*. He, flogged, sneered and mocked, slapped, spit on, pierced, denied, and condemned, did not allow what was happening to Him cause Him to resist His crucifiers. Take a look at Jesus's actions on the cross in regard to *forgetting, remembering, and reaching.*

(1) Forgetting: Luke 23:34 – "And Jesus prayed, Father, forgive them, for they know not what they do. And they divided His garments *and* distributed them by casting lots for them." Jesus, in agonizing pain, looked down on the murderous crowd and prayed for them. Not only did He pray for the people crucifying Him, His prayer was also for you and me. Keep in mind, forgetting and forgiving are kindred spirits. Jesus prayed for the religious leaders and the bloodthirsty mob that were determined to crucify Him. The mob probably understood what they were doing, but they did not foresee the chain of historical events they were setting in motion. Nor did

they understand the full extent
of their wickedness, or that
Jesus was the Messiah, whom
they were expecting according
to prophecy. They were blinded
with hatred and did not know
they were crucifying the King of
glory! While on the cross, Jesus
was forgetting about Himself,
interceding on behalf of the
people, pleading to His Heavenly
Father to forgive them.

Jesus prayed to the Father to forgive the
murderers while they were crucifying Him. This is the
ultimate expression of forgetting and forgiving while
remembering His mission as He prayed to the Father
to receive Him in glory. Jesus expressed His love,
grace, and mercy for the people without expecting
anything from them in return. It is understandable to
argue that Jesus's love and forgiveness is greater than
what we can do. I beg to differ, and so does Jesus!

Stephen was a mortal human being, just like
you and me, a servant of the Lord who was stoned
to death simply because he told the people the truth.
I encourage you to read the entire events that led up

to his death, but here's the climactic account of his death recorded in Acts 7:54-60:

> Now upon hearing these things, they [the Jews] were cut to the heart *and* infuriated, and they ground their teeth against [Stephen]. But he, full of the Holy Spirit *and* controlled by Him, gazed into heaven and saw the glory (the splendor and majesty) of God, and Jesus standing at God's right hand; And he said, Look! **I** see the heavens opened, and the Son of man standing at God's right hand! But they raised a great shout and put their hands over their ears and rushed together upon him. Then they dragged him out of the city and began to stone him, and the witnesses placed their garments at the feet of a young man named Saul. [Compare Acts 22:20.] And while they were stoning Stephen, he prayed, Lord Jesus, receive *and*

accept *and* welcome my spirit! And falling on his knees, he cried out loudly, Lord, fix not this sin upon them (lay it not to their charge]! And when he had said this, he fell asleep [in death].

When filled with the Holy Ghost, *forgetting, remembering, and reaching* are not only what we should do, it is what we are empowered with the love of Christ to do. Listen! Before Jesus gave up the ghost, He cried with a loud voice. Before Stephen fell asleep in Christ, he also cried with a loud voice. Jesus and Stephen took their last breaths, praying for the people who were crucifying or stoning them. Most striking of all, Jesus was standing at the right hand of God, cheering for Stephen as he was being stoned to death. Not only did Jesus personally understand what Stephen was experiencing at the hands of his accusers, but He knew it was the love of God that gave him the strength to endure without complaining or condemning. Stephen asked God to forgive the people who were stoning him to death!

Is it not also strange that Saul, who was present and consented to the stoning of Stephen, was chosen by Christ to continue Stephen's ministry that led to him being stoned to death? Shortly thereafter, Ananias received from Christ the following instructions concerning Saul, "But the Lord said to him, Go, this man is a chosen instrument of Mine to bear My name before the Gentiles and kings and the descendants of Israel. For I will make clear to him how much he will be afflicted and suffer for My name's sake." (Acts 9:1-16).

Saul the persecutor became apostle Paul the persecuted. The person he was is not the person he was transformed into being. We are blessed, and can be a blessing because God is He "Who gives life to the dead and speaks of the nonexistent things that [He has foretold and promised] as if they [already] existed" [Compare Acts 4:17b]. For example, what we may see as small, unimportant acorns, God sees as a forest of tall and powerful oak trees. The person Saul was before he met Jesus on the Damascus road should help us to understand why Paul was always forgetting those things behind and reaching forth to those things that were before him. Paul, in fact, lived his entire Christian life pressing forward toward the mark for the prize of the high or upward calling of God in Christ Jesus.

Use the following points as a personal inventory of your calling and purpose:

1. You are not beyond God's reach
2. God has a plan for your life
3. Do not give up on yourself
4. You are not hopeless or useless
5. Do not give up on others
6. They are not hopeless or useless

(2) Remembering: John 12:27 – "Now My soul is troubled *and* distressed, and what shall **I** say? Father, save Me from this hour [of trial and agony]? But it was for this very purpose that **I** have come to this hour [that **I** might undergo it]." Jesus's mission is also affirmed in Luke 19:10, "For the Son of Man came to seek and to save that which was lost." Jesus demonstrated how to stay focused on your focus is on making your calling your focused purpose. Jesus's *agape* love for the human race empowered Him to look beyond the cross and the unwillingness of the people to come unto Him.

The uncompromising willingness to stay the course is possible when forgetting and remembering are working together as kindred disciplines. The willingness to forget the past means you are not remembering what you are committed to forgetting. It is an act of love to forget a wrong suffered, rather than to remember it in an unforgiving and revengeful way. When lovingly and thoughtfully remembering what to forget, you are also challenging yourself to forget to remember unprofitable experiences, praying for the obedience and courage to forget. You have to remember the past before you can forget it and put it to rest. To discharge the past from active duty is to retire it with solemn respect. It will prove rewarding if filed away as lessons learned when the past is surrendered in the hands of *forgetting, remembering, and reaching*.

(3) Reaching: Luke 23:46 – "And Jesus, crying out with a loud voice, said, Father, into Your hands **I** commit My spirit! And with these words, He expired." [Compare Ps. 31:5.] Jesus was reaching for and accepting His reason for coming into this world unto His own. He reached the summit of his mission. He was crucified, descended into the lower parts of the earth, was resurrected, and ascended to heaven, where He is now seated at the right hand of the Father in glory.

For you and me, reaching for the blessed promises of God requires stretching ourselves beyond our present level of maturity. We must be willing to forgive and forget. It is therefore no small wonder that reaching and growing are challenging, to say the least. They require complete faithfulness and obedience. The willingness and the courage to be tested and exposed, to be hurt by others, is part of the process. Reaching also requires letting go of what you are holding onto, embracing the changes and challenges that lie ahead. This is difficult to do when what you are reaching for is entangled with what you are trying to forget. What if, for example, you are reaching for the strength to forgive your spouse for something he or she is continuing to do? Your reaching will likely be hindered and disrupted. It is extremely hard to forget to remember the past that is part of the present.

For example, Hosea's relationship with his wife Gomer and God's relationship with the children of Israel are perfect examples of *forgetting, remembering, and reaching.* Gomer was unfaithful to her husband, Hosea, and Israel to their God. Despite their whoredom, Hosea remained faithful to Gomer and God to the children of Israel. It was unconditional love that prevailed over unfaithfulness and whoredom.

Neither Hosea nor God deserved the betrayal and unfaithfulness that they endured. Before considering what Hosea went through, or what you and I are going through, let's pause for a moment, and look at the little picture through the spiritual lens of the big picture shared by the apostle Paul in Romans 8:18, ["But what of that?] For **I** consider that the sufferings of this present time (this present life) are not worth being compared with the glory that is about to be revealed to us *and* in us *and* for us *and* conferred on us!"

When, and not if, we are going *through,* never forget to remember that temporal suffering will precede eternal glory. What we endure in this present life will yield the faithful everlasting rewards in the everlasting glory of God. On the other hand, some suffering in this life is self-inflicted. Nonetheless, God preordained and singled you out in eternity past to fulfill your calling. Be thankful God called, justified, and glorified you to do a work that He chose you to do from the foundation of the world.

Finally, the total of our lives rests on reaching for the miraculous by trusting God beyond our own understanding. The apostle Paul said it best in Philippians 1:6, "And **I** am convinced *and* sure of this very thing, that He who began a good work in you will continue until the day of Jesus Christ [right up to the time of His return], developing [that good work] *and* perfecting *and* bringing it to full completion in you."

Forgetting, remembering, and reaching require focusing, focusing, focusing! Therefore, continue reaching, reaching, reaching!

Chapter 11

The Miraculous Power of
Love is Unstoppable

The thirteenth chapter of First Corinthians is affectionately called the love chapter, and love it is! Not so much a definition of love, but an expression of what love does and does not do, that love is as love does. Of equal importance, the entire Bible is a love letter from God the Father, written by God the Holy Spirit, delivered to us by God the Son. The Bible reveals the outpouring of God's love for humanity, with each of us on His mind and in His heart.

The entire chapter is being discussed from the point of view of *forgetting, remembering, and reaching.*

1. **Forgetting: 1 Corinthians 13:1-3** – If I [can] speak in the tongues of men and [even] of angels, but have not love (that reasoning, intentional, spiritual devotion such as is inspired by God's love for and in us), I am only a noisy gong or a clanging cymbal. And if I have prophetic powers (the gift of interpreting the divine will and purpose), and understand all the secret truths *and* mysteries and possess all knowledge, and if I have [sufficient] faith so that I can remove mountains, but have not love (God's love in me), I am nothing (a useless nobody). Even if I dole out all that I have [to the poor in providing] food, and if I surrender my body to be burned *or in order that I may glory,* but have not love (God's love in me), I gain nothing.

Paul was neither bragging nor trusting his achievements to prove who he was. On the other hand, neither was he complaining. Paul was reminding his audience that the most extraordinary gifts used, services rendered, and sacrifices offered that are not grounded and rooted in the love of Christ, are equal to a total of nothing. Paul was forgetting his accomplishments and failures. They did not justify, qualify, or disqualify who he was. He was admitting that his gifts, talents, and faith were virtually useless if not grounded and rooted in love. He was also warning that it is possible to do good and righteous deeds that are not the righteousness of God. Paul refused to make noise stressing who he was or what he had done or was doing. He was committed to forgetting his accomplishments and to loving others without expecting praise or rewards in return. He did not prequalify whom he would serve or love based on their credentials or treatment of him. He was willing to love regardless of what anyone else did or did not do. Paul was committed to forgetting his past successes and failures.

An Openhearted Questionnaire

You are being asked to answer a number of self-examination questions. It is a questionnaire designed to reveal truth or untruth as opposed to right or wrong answers. Reflect on your responses and confess your answers to God so you can hear yourself admitting your responses to Him. But this questionnaire is for your benefit, not God's. God will not reveal to you things that you want to know, but are unwilling to obey for His glory.

Read the following questions, and do a self-check to determine where you are, insofar as truth and untruth are concerned.

a. How many people are you holding grudges against?

b. Did you get upset when a driver refused to yield the right-of-way to you at an intersection?

c. Did a coworker block a promotion, raise, or better job?

d. Did a trusted friend betray you?

e. Did a close friend have a love affair with your spouse, or damage a relationship with someone you love deeply?

f. Did a friend refuse to repay a loan as promised?

g. Have you done any of these things to anyone?

h. If so, do you want them to forgive you?

Your answers are more about truth and untruth rather than right and wrong, though it is always wrong not to do right, and it is never right to do wrong.

But with these questions, you can identify whether your answers are truthful or untruthful. You have personally experienced or witnessed how easy it is to become upset over much of nothing? If you believe you have never lied or done anything unbecoming your entire life, you have likely learned how to look through or around the plank in your eye, though not likely. In any event, you are the only person who needs to know your answers. Your responses will help you to clearly see you, and identify to what degree you are *forgetting, remembering, and reaching.*

But forget about yourself for a moment, and reflect on Jesus and Stephen. In reality, they experienced much more than what this questionnaire will reveal. What you and I are experiencing are *small potatoes* in comparison to what they endured. We have not been physically crucified, stoned to death, or martyred. Jesus and Stephen forgave the people, not after the fact, but during the very act of being crucified and stoned, and for good reasons. Love responded to hate with love. Jesus is the resurrection and the life, the Lamb of God, and absolutely nothing has any power over Him. Stephen was absolutely certain Christ would resurrect him, for hate had no power over him.

Insofar as you and I are concerned, any unwillingness on our part to forgive is unforgivable and inexcusable! With man it is impossible to overcome hate with love, but with God it is not only possible, but forgiving is doable! It is our reasonable or rational service, and remembering plays a vital part in the process.

2. **Remembering: 1 Corinthians 13:4–8 –** Love endures long *and* is patient and kind; love never is envious *nor* boils over with jealousy, is not boastful *or* vainglorious, does not display itself haughtily. It is not conceited (arrogant and inflated with pride); it is not rude (unmannerly) *and* does not act unbecomingly. Love (God's love in us) does not insist on its own rights *or* its own way, *for* it is not self-seeking; it is not touchy *or* fretful *or* resentful; it takes no account of the evil done to it [it pays no attention to a suffered wrong]. It does not rejoice at injustice *and* unrighteousness, but rejoices when right *and* truth prevail. Love bears up under anything *and* everything that comes, is ever ready to believe the best of every person, its hopes are fadeless under

all circumstances, and it endures everything [without weakening]. Love never fails [never fades out or becomes obsolete or comes to an end]. As for prophecy (the gift of interpreting the divine will and purpose), it will be fulfilled *and* pass away; as for tongues, they will be destroyed *and* cease; as for knowledge, it will pass away [it will lose its value and be superseded by truth].

In these verses, the apostle Paul wasn't selfishly focusing on himself. He was forgetting himself and the things he had accomplished or suffered the loss of. He was remembering what love does and does not do. *Agape* love does not give up or give out when the going gets tough. *Agape* love does not throw in the towel when the people you are committed to love and serve are plotting to kill or destroy you.

Please do not forget this truth: remembering has positive and negative qualities. Remembering to forget a wrong suffered is an act of love. Remembering not to forget to love unconditionally is our reasonable or rational service. It is important to know how to forget to remember, and how to remember to forget. The words forgetting and remembering are used back and forth in ways that may seem confusing. It is therefore critically important to discuss and clarify why they are used in so many different ways.

Most important of all, love is a powerful force that overcomes hate and all its cohorts. Love desires and works untiringly and unselfishly to build others up with little or no concern of personal sacrifices or losses. When confronted with hatred or hostility, love flourishes all the more. Love never forgets to remember memories to hold onto, but forgets everything that is not worth remembering. Love is an attribute of God that empowers the believer with the strength to filter out or retain memories without regrets or expectations. Keep in mind, love is as love does, and remembering whether to remember or not is key to receiving the blessed promises of God.

3. **Reaching: 1 Corinthians 13:9-13** – For our knowledge is fragmentary (incomplete and imperfect), and our prophecy (our teaching) is fragmentary (incomplete and fragmentary). But when the complete *and* perfect (total) comes, the incomplete *and* imperfect will vanish away (become antiquated, void, and superseded). When I was a child, **I** talked like a child, **I** thought

like a child, I reasoned like a child; now that **I** have become a man, **I** am done with childish ways *and* have put them aside. For now we are looking in a mirror that gives only a dim (blurred) reflection [of reality as in a riddle or enigma], but then [when perfection comes] we shall see in reality *and* face to face! Now **I** know in part (imperfectly), but then **I** shall know *and* understand fully *and* clearly, even in the same manner as **I** have been fully *and* clearly known *and* understood [by God]. And so faith, hope, love abide [faith– conviction and belief respecting man's relation to God and divine things; hope–joyful and confident expectation of eternal salvation; love–true affection for God and man, growing out of God's love for and in us], these three; but the greatest of these is love.

The uniting of reaching and receiving are kindred actions, likened to walking and swinging the arms at the same time in perfect rhythm. The two are also as dependent on each other as inhaling and exhaling are to breathing. You can, for example, choose not to inhale, exhale, or breathe for a short time. You can refuse to receive and complete the love cycle of *forgetting, remembering, and reaching.* However, reaching out and receiving are most attainable when joined with forgetting and remembering.

Reaching is also an act of pressing forward, confronting the forces determined to stop you. You can compare pressing to that of overcoming the winds of adversity that will attack you through your mind, or the mind of someone else. Your trials and tribulations may be chasing you from the outside in or from the inside out. We sometimes fail to reach our full spiritual potential because we reject instructions and corrections.

An important key to reaching full spiritual potential is to recognize it is an ongoing journey. Are you ready and willing to receive everything God has for you? It is a matter of knowing we do not know everything about ourselves, and even less about God. The mirror of our heart is not as enlightened, or as pure as it will be when we see God face to face. Also, reaching and letting go are part of a single act connected with forgetting and remembering. You cannot forget without forgiving. You cannot forgive without remembering what to forget, and you cannot be reaching if you are not forgetting. If you are gripping the past and your mind is unwilling to embrace the present, you are unprepared for the future that always reveals itself today.

Receiving and reaching full potential are inseparably connected with growth and maturity. Adults who pout and have temper tantrums like little children are likely not reaching and pressing toward the mark for the high or upward calling of God in Christ Jesus. Adults must guard against becoming aged children! It is common practice for children to dress and act older than their age. Some adults dress and act in ways that make them appear younger than their age. The young use makeup and getups to look older than they are. Some adults choose plastic surgery, facelifts, nose and lip surgery, and liposuction, to name a few procedures, to look younger than they are. Young people want to be adults until they discover adulthood leads to old age, and the decline in health is chaperoned by time and aging.

Most people want to go to heaven, but they would rather not die to get there. Everyone wants to live a long time, but does not look forward to getting old and dealing with the challenges of old age. My pastor, before he transitions from this life, came to an honest but realistic conclusion: "Getting old is a blessing, but it is sure inconvenient." One reason we want to get out of this life alive is that we know it wasn't God's will for us to die in the first place. So, whether you are young or old, expect Jesus to return during your lifetime. Therefore, prepare to live and not die, and have the faith to live life by *forgetting, remembering, and reaching.*

We know, according to Hebrews 11:1 that **"NOW FAITH** is the assurance (the confirmation, the title deed) of the things [we] hope for, being the proof of things [we] do not see *and* the conviction of their reality [faith perceiving as real fact what is not revealed to the senses"]. Moreover, Romans 5:5 assures us that "Such hope never disappoints *or* deludes *or* shames us, for God's love has been poured out in our hearts through the Holy Spirit Who has been given to us."

We cannot please God without having faith in Him, but God Himself does not do the things He do by having faith in Himself, per se. God does not need faith to do the things He does. He is God, faithful to His Word. In Hebrews 11:3, it is written, "By faith we understand that the worlds [during the successive ages] were framed (fashioned, put in order, and equipped for their intended purpose) by the word of God, so that what we see was not made out of things which are visible." And in Hebrews 6:13 it is also written, "For when God made [His] promise to Abraham, He swore by Himself, since He had no one greater by whom to swear." In Isaiah 14:24 and Hebrews 6:17, it is written, "The Lord of hosts has sworn, saying, Surely, as **I** have thought *and* planned, so shall it come to pass, and as **I** have purposed, so shall it stand. Accordingly, God also, in His desire to show more convincingly *and* beyond doubt to those who were to inherit the promise the unchangeableness of His purpose *and* plan, intervened (mediated) with an oath." The Word of God needs no validation from anyone or anything. It is the Word of God and Jesus is the Word made flesh.

In the first chapter of Genesis it is documented that in the beginning whatever God said, God did. It is also recorded in John 1:1 "**IN THE** beginning [before all time] was the Word (Christ), and the Word was with God, and the Word was God Himself." [Compare Isa. 9:6]. To have faith in something or someone is to depend on and trust someone greater than self. We cannot say God, who is the Source and Supplier of faith, has faith in anything or anyone outside of or beyond Himself. All we can say is that God is faithful to His Word, and we are to have in the faithfulness of God to His Word.

What do you do to keep your heart beating or your eyes seeing? You do absolutely nothing. Your eyes and heart, in fact, your entire body, function according to the will of God without any help from you, though living a healthy lifestyle is something that you can do. But let's change course and consider hope, faith, and love: The greatest of the three is love, and God Himself is love. He did not create His creation with faith or hope. He is God, and love is as love does. God spoke, and the power of His love caused what He spoke to be.

It is His love that holds all of creation in its place and causes it to function according to His divine will. Mankind, the most marvelous of God's creation, can go to God when we transgress. God Himself forgives us our sins and shortcomings. When we repent, He casts them into the sea of forgetfulness. He is therefore long-suffering, and His grace and mercy move Him to withhold His wrath. God remembers His oath that He made with Himself. God reaches down to us through Jesus's sacrifice on the cross. If we did not have the indwelling presence of the Holy Spirit in the world living in the believer, we would have been destroyed long ago! God Himself is *forgetting, remembering, and reaching.* What about us? We, all the more, are to live life by *forgetting, remembering, and reaching.*

The Ending of This Book is Your Beginning

We are nearing the end of *Forgetting, Remembering, Reaching,* but there is much more that can be said about the importance of *forgetting, remembering, and reaching.* So, what final words can be said? Throughout this book, the focus has been mostly on you and me. The focus will shortly shift more to God, our Creator, and His love for us. But a quick glimpse back on humanity is a reminder and warning that you can't conquer what you won't confront.

God forgets past sins that we have repented of. He remembers His promise to never leave or forsake us. He reaches down and embraces us in His loving arms of grace and mercy. He showers us with unmerited favor and divine enablement. We, on the other hand, may struggle with *forgetting, remembering, and reaching.* We must therefore commit to entrusting our lives to God. We are to obey Him and learn to make the important distinction between forgetting to remember and remembering to forget. You are encouraged to learn to reach out to God by remembering to forget trials and tribulations while forgetting to remember the people who committed them. At the sweet or bitter end of life in this life, the only thing that matters is that God is *forgetting, remembering, and reaching* down to us. Begin or continue from where you are, and God will take you to where He desires you to be. Probably the most difficult stumbling block to *forgetting, remembering, and reaching* is not *forgetting, remembering, and reaching*. It is accepting by faith God's firm and uncompromising commitment to *forgetting, remembering, and reaching* down to us.

I pray that *Forgetting, Remembering, Reaching* will help you practice what you have learned, and trust the Holy Spirit to teach you much more than what you will read in this book. But one final word about sin, that is often the offspring of not *forgetting, remembering, and reaching*. Do not forget to remember that sin has an insatiable appetite, but it does not a stomach. Sin can never satisfy it's sinful appetite for more sin. Sin lusting for more sin grows in proportion with the sin that it is fed.

Sinning, in many ways, can be likened to jumping off a tall building. It's not the jump but the landing that kills. Sin and sinning may feel good and satisfying during the act. The deathblow or the consequences are not always payable or due on the front-end. But when lust has conceived, it brings forth sin, and sin, when it is finished, brings forth death. Sinning is to falling out of grace as jumping from a tall building is to falling to the ground.

You have an opportunity to begin or to continue with a renewed sense of commitment by living this lifelong journey by *forgetting, remembering, and reaching*. In the closing pages of this book, selective verses from I Corinthians 13, the *love* chapter, are revisited.

Chapter 12

The Power of Love

Let's Do It Again

As the end of *Forgetting, Remembering, Reaching* grows even closer, it is expedient to revisit in its closing pages verses from the previous chapter. Therefore selective verses from I Corinthians 13, affectionately called the love chapter, are among the closing pages of this book.

> Love endures long *and* is patient
> and kind; love never is envious
> *nor* boils over with jealousy, is
> not boastful *or* vainglorious,

does not display itself haughtily. It is not conceited (arrogant and inflated with pride); it is not rude (unmannerly *and* does not act unbecomingly. Love (God's love in us) does not insist on its own rights *or* its own way, *for* it is not self-seeking; it is not touchy *or* fretful *or* resentful; it takes no account of the evil done to it [it pays no attention to a suffered wrong. It does not rejoice at injustice *and* unrighteousness, but rejoices when right *and* truth prevail. Love bears up under anything *and* everything that comes, is ever ready to believe the best of every person, its hopes are fadeless under all circumstances, and it endures everything [without weakening] [Compare I Cor. 13:4-7].

The following points summarize the power of love. Let's do it again is to allow love to do as love does:

1. Love is a two-way power
2. Love reciprocates and gives back to itself through people who love
3. Love is meant to give
4. Love flows and goes, gives and takes, compromises and sacrifices
5. The Holy Spirit is often referred to as the Wind
6. You can, to some degree, reject or ignore the Holy Spirit, but you cannot prevent Him from doing what He does
7. Love can be rejected, but you cannot prevent love from moving searchingly throughout the universe, especially in search of receptive hearts and vessels of honor
8. Love compromises, not that it violates itself, but rather it gives for the benefit and betterment of others without selfishly exercising its rights, but willingly and joyfully sacrifices itself
9. The essence of sacrifice is exemplified in Matthew 26:53: Jesus said, "Do you suppose that I cannot appeal to My Father,

and He will immediately provide Me with more than twelve legions [more than 80,000] of angels?"

10. Love is power under the control of the Holy Spirit, who is our Source of Power

11. Love stays in its metaphoric lane, and often yields its will-of-the-way to others

12. Love allows others to respond with love

13. Love is never out of order

14. Love respects, listens, gives, forgives, forgets, and moves forward toward noble ideas with excellent and exceptional courage

15. Love is limitless and always open to sharing, caring, looking beyond what was and seeing what is

16. Love looks for open doors of opportunity to reach out to others, not just in times of need, but as an ongoing expression of its boundless capacity to put the needs of others above its own

17. Love is not a guest, but a servant

18. Love does not seek rewards and recognition

19. Love blesses others in secrecy, and God rewards openly

20. Love's reward is in giving itself away to others

21. Love does not prequalify who deserves to be loved
22. Love disempowers hate. Grace invades the forces of evil with unmerited favor and divine enablement
23. Love is committed to reaching the unreachable, loving the unloving, forgiving the unforgiving, and helping the helpless
24. Love bridges the chasms of indifference and intolerance
25. Love is fail-proof
26. Love is irrepressible, undefeatable, irrefutable, and self-sustainable
27. Love is as love does
28. Love is selfless, and giving empowers love to give more of its inexhaustible self
29. Love is a selfless and passionate fire, consuming and annihilating its enemies as it spreads from heart to heart, house to house, neighborhood to neighborhood, and from states to countries throughout the entire world
30. Love forgets to remember and remembers to forget
31. Love is God, and God is love
32. May God continue to bless you richly!

Epilogue

The word epilogue is defined as "a concluding section that rounds out the design of a literary work." This definition consummates the writing of *Forgetting, Remembering, Reaching* by sharing God's love story. Although the love of God is unparalleled with any other story ever written, it does share certain similarities with love stories, whether fact or fiction. In the Bible, God's love story covers every facet of life. There are highs and lows, separations, estrangements, and reconciliations. Sacrifice and betrayal perfectly illustrate love shared or offered by the Giver to the receiver, which is not always a smooth transition. Yet the power and the heartbeat of God's creation are grounded and rooted in His love for all of His creation. The power of love and our obsession with love is the underlying theme of almost every song, movie, and storyline, whether biblical or unbiblical, though love is often portrayed in perverse, violent, and unbiblical ways.

Therefore, regardless of the varied subject matters in this book, its ultimate message is that God loves you. Love may seem missing in the Bible in a chapter or two, here and there. But if you commit to read verses or chapters before and after the verses and chapters read, the love of God is the message or the picture behind the picture. While the object of His love does and often goes astray, everything God does is to redeem the object of His love back to Himself.

Pick up your Bible and flip to a page, any page, and read the verse that reaches out to you. If love seems missing, read verses or even chapters before and after that verse or chapter, and you will see that the love of God is crying out to humanity. What if you opened your Bible to John 3:16? God is revealing a sacrifice made for you before you were born, separated from Him. He wants you to know that He sacrificed His only Son so that you could live. Jesus died so you could live forevermore. He came to seek and to save you, to reach out to you even when you were rejecting and running away from Him. His love for you has endured and will endure and overcome everything that is trying to woo you away from Him. God's love story, lovingly and accurately shared in the Bible, begins and ends in victory. Everything that happens between Genesis 1:1 and Revelation 22:21 is the sum total of His love story to, about, and for you.

Read, study, and reflect on God's message to you in the Bible. Whenever you don't understand what He is saying or what He means, ask the Holy Spirit to help you. He wants you to clearly understand everything that God is saying to you. Learn to listen, obey, and beware of the consequences that befall everyone who does not listen and obey Him. He tells you in His letter, over and over, how much He loves you, revealing present and future plans for you. In many relationships, the promise to love forever is short-lived. God's promise, unlike promises made by man, is unbreakable, irrefutable, undeniable, irreversible, and everlasting.

Should you feel unloved or unappreciated along life's journey, stop and take time to read your love letter. You will at once know that God is looking out for you because He loves you with an everlasting love. The Bible is written for everyone in general but to and for you in particular! On a personal and experiential level, I now know that the writing of this book, *Forgetting, Remembering, Reaching*, was first of all ordained by God to help guide me through surprising, yet unsurprising transitions.

In closing, I now understand, like never before, the importance of *forgetting, remembering, and reaching*. Take this journey with me and forget the hurt, the disappointments, betrayals, and the abandonment of family and friends.

While it is needful to forget all of that and more, remember and cherish the lessons learned and the wisdom attained that is grounded and rooted in unmasking the truth of God, working mightily in the seemingly veiled shadows of His brilliant glory. The ultimate lesson learned is that the work God is doing in you and me cannot be attributed to human effort, ingenuity, or the will of man, regardless of who we are in Him. All the glory, praise, and adoration belong to God and Him alone. God is removing from our lives everyone and everything that causes us to look to them more than to Him. He had to subtract from our lives before adding and multiplying His abundant grace and mercy. His unmerited peace, prosperity, purpose, and positioning are being personified in your life for you to reach your place of authority in Him.

This book is written especially for you because you are reading the very last words of it.

Peace Abide.

Amen.